### Stunned, she looked to Landon, who smiled and said, "Hello, Jadin."

She felt a jolt. It was like the fizzle of electricity from a faulty switch—the same jolt that had passed between them on their first meeting eight years ago. Hot slivers of lightning heated Jadin to the bone, bringing a flush to her cheeks and a tingle to certain parts of her anatomy that no other glance had reached—not even with Michael.

*What on earth is the matter with me?* she wondered.

As calmly as she could manage, Jadin walked up to him, ignoring the beautiful bouquet of red roses he offered. At six foot three, Landon towered over her. "What exactly did you hope to gain by coming here? We both agreed that the marriage was a mistake, which is why we had it dissolved."

"That is precisely *why* I came," he responded. "Jadin, we're still married. The divorce never happened."

Landon appeared to be enjoying her struggle to capture her composure. "I don't believe you." She could feel the electric heat coursing through her as if his sensual energy was powering up hers.

*Not now*, she told herself. *I can't think of him in that way.*

Dear Reader,

Have you ever made an impulsive decision, and once you thought about it, you realized that it might have been a mistake? In *Another Chance with You*, Jadin DuGrandpre does just that. However, that decision comes back to haunt her five years later when Landon Trent comes to Charleston, South Carolina.

Just when Jadin thinks she has found the perfect man to spend the rest of her life with, Landon is back with the announcement that they are still married. He proposes that they live as man and wife for a year before finalizing their divorce.

I hope you will enjoy this fourth installment of the DuGrandpres of Charleston series. I really had a lot of fun writing this story about soul mates who are destined to be together and live happily-ever-after.

As always, thank you for reading my stories. I appreciate your support and I thank you for twenty-one years and seventy-seven books. I could not have done it without you—my readers!

Best regards,

*Jacquelin Thomas*

# ANOTHER CHANCE WITH *You*

# JACQUELIN THOMAS

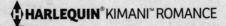

HARLEQUIN® KIMANI™ ROMANCE

Recycling programs
for this product may
not exist in your area.

ISBN-13: 978-1-335-21696-0

Another Chance with You

Copyright © 2018 by Jacquelin Thomas

**Printed in U.S.A.**

**Jacquelin Thomas** is an award-winning, bestselling author with more than fifty-five books in print. When not writing, she is busy catching up on her reading, attending sporting events and spoiling her grandchildren. Jacquelin and her family live in North Carolina.

### Books by Jacquelin Thomas

### Harlequin Kimani Romance

*Five Star Attraction*
*Five Star Temptation*
*Legal Attraction*
*Five Star Romance*
*Five Star Seduction*
*Styles of Seduction*
*Wrangling Wes*
*Five Star Desire*
*Forever My Baby*
*Only for You*
*Return to Me*

Visit the Author Profile page
at Harlequin.com for more titles.

# Chapter 1

Jadin DuGrandpre glanced at the dazzling diamond engagement ring on her left hand. She and Michael had been dating for three years, with the last two being long-distance. Although she was twenty-nine years old, she hoped her parents would be supportive of her relocating to California to be with the man she planned to marry.

Whenever she thought of leaving Charleston, her home, her family, Jadin felt a sharp ache in her heart. She would never tell Michael, but she had mixed feelings about moving so far away.

Her twin sister, Jordin, was having twins in a couple of months, and her brother, Austin, was also expecting a baby—Jadin really did not want to miss these family milestones.

She pulled into the driveway of her parents' home, eager to show off her engagement ring.

Jordin parked behind her and got out.

"I didn't know that was you," Jadin said, eyeing the SUV. "New car?"

Placing her hand on her swollen belly, Jordin responded, "Yeah. Ethan read that Volvo was rated one of the safest automobiles, so he bought me one."

"That's so wonderful. He wants to keep you and the babies safe." Jadin loved that her brother-in-law was so protective of Jordin and his children. It was very sweet. She wondered briefly if Michael would be like that when they started a family.

"I appreciate it, but at times, I feel like he's smothering me," Jordin confessed. "When we found out that I was carrying twins…girl, he hardly let me out of his sight."

Jadin laughed. "He wouldn't even let you drive to work for almost a week."

"He got over that real quick," Jordin responded with a chuckle. "I made him drive me all over town."

"How are you feeling?"

"I'm glad I'm ten weeks from delivering. I love being pregnant, but I'm ready to see and hold my babies."

"I can't wait to meet my nieces or nephews…or niece and nephew…"

"I wanted to know what we're having, but Ethan wanted to be surprised. Bree and Ashton are having a gender-reveal party next month. I hope they're having a little girl, because Emery has been asking for a sister."

As they neared the steps leading to the porch, Jordin asked her sister, "I'm kind of surprised to see you here. Michael's in town, right?"

Jadin nodded. "He got in last night."

"Is he still pressuring you to move to California?"

"Yeah, he wants me to move out there. This time he gave a very convincing argument for why I should." Jadin waved her fingers. "Notice anything different?"

Jordin's mouth dropped open. "You're engaged... Oh, wow... I'm... I agree... That's a very persuasive reason to relocate."

"I think Mom will be happy for me, but I'm not so sure about Daddy. Marrying Michael means I'll be leaving the firm." Jadin had remained awake most of the night, thinking about what accepting Michael's proposal meant for her. When she graduated law school, she was fine with being away from her family. But now she felt conflicted. She enjoyed the family gatherings, spending time with her nieces and nephews. She wanted to watch them grow up. All that would change when she and Michael got married.

"This is *your* life, sis," Jordin said. "If for some reason Ethan decided to leave Charleston—I'm not going to give it a second thought. As much as I'd miss everyone, my home is with him."

"I don't think that Ethan would ever ask you to leave, though. He knows how close we are as a family."

"You're right."

"Austin suggested that I propose opening a second law office in California to Daddy."

"I actually think it's a great idea—if that's what you want to do. For now, just focus on your engagement. Planning a wedding can be overwhelming." She scanned her sister's face. "Are you sure about this?"

"Yes." Jadin gave a nervous chuckle. "The first hurdle will be telling the parents."

"Well, there's no time like right now—that sparkly ring's gonna give it away as soon as we walk into the house."

Landon Trent sat inside his car, air-conditioning blowing to ward off the May heat for what seemed like hours, although it was only more like fifteen minutes. This was his first time coming to the DuGrandpre estate. He'd heard so much about it when he and Jadin dated in law school, but the opportunity to visit never materialized.

One Christmas, Landon was supposed to join Jadin and her family for the holidays, but he lost his mother that year. A sharp pain sliced through his heart, where grief still existed.

He never would have finished law school if it had not been for his uncle Tim and Jadin's love and support. Landon glanced down at the wedding band on his left hand. He had come to Charleston to reclaim his wife. He and Jadin had eloped while in Las Vegas to celebrate their graduation.

The Secret Service had recruited him his last year in law school, a decision Jadin had initially supported, but then she'd blindsided Landon by asking for a divorce.

He had agreed with her that they had rushed into the marriage without much forethought, but the more Landon considered ending the marriage, the more his heart ached at the thought of losing Jadin.

Her cousin had just lost her husband and Jadin was afraid of losing him in the same way. However, Landon was committed to the Secret Service and that was not going to change, so Jadin went home to Charleston and he left for FLETC, the Federal Law Enforcement Training Center in Georgia.

He spent his first two years investigating computer and telecommunications fraud and other violations. Then he was presented an opportunity for protective detail. As time went on, Landon did not see any benefits from the endless overtime travel and continuing from one assignment to another without a break—his marriage never would've survived the disruptions that would have come with his job. Landon could have gone back to investigation detail but had chosen to fight for his marriage instead. He'd secured a job as the deputy prosecutor in Charleston.

He glanced up at the house. Several cars were parked in the driveway. Landon considered that the DuGrandpres were entertaining guests, but he refused to let that deter him. Not reaching out to Jadin had been hard, but Landon did not want to give her any advance notice. He wanted the world to know that Jadin DuGrandpre was still his wife.

This was not the way he'd initially planned to confront her, but last night changed everything. He had been at a restaurant having dinner, when Jadin walked in with her date.

It was clear she only had eyes for the man she was with. Consumed with jealousy, Landon had briefly considered interrupting their romantic evening, but then her date pulled out a ring and proposed.

He'd followed them back to her place. It had been pure torture knowing that she wanted to spend her life with another man. Landon swallowed the feelings of betrayal he felt—he had no right to feel this way. Jadin was the innocent one in this situation, he reminded himself. She had no idea what was coming for her—that he was coming for her.

Landon had stayed in surveillance mode, finally leaving after 2:00 a.m. and returning at the break of dawn. He'd followed Jadin to her parents' house, leaving to pick up flowers from a nearby florist on Sullivan's Island before returning to the estate.

It was time for him to reclaim his wife.

Jadin stuck her hand in her pocket, her fingers toying with the engagement ring. She could hardly wait to share the news that she was marrying Michael. She had asked him to come with her to break the news, but he refused, saying that it was something she should do alone. Jadin did not understand his logic, but that was just Michael.

"Aunt Rochelle, I didn't know you'd be here," Jordin said as she sank down into an overstuffed chair in the family room.

Jadin had hoped to tell Jordin, Austin and their parents first. She loved her aunt dearly, but the woman would be blabbing about the engagement before Jadin had a chance to make it home.

"I just came by to go over the details for the Heart Association fund-raiser. Eleanor and I are cochairing the event this year."

Jadin stole a peek at her mother's face, bit back a smile and sent up a silent prayer. She was about to take a seat beside her sister when she heard a familiar voice in the foyer.

She gasped in surprise. "It can't be…"

"Jadin, what is this man talking about?" her father

asked, bursting into the room with a younger man following behind. "He says that he's your husband."

"What's wrong, Etienne?" Eleanor looked at her daughter. *"Husband?"*

"Mom…I can explain everything."

Stunned, she looked to Landon, who smiled and said, "Hello, Jadin."

She felt a jolt. It was like the fizzle of electricity from a faulty switch—the same jolt that had passed between them on their first meeting eight years ago. Hot slivers of lightning heated Jadin to the bone, bringing a flush to her cheeks and a tingle to certain parts of her anatomy that no other glance had reached—not even with Michael.

*What on earth is the matter with me?* she wondered.

As calmly as she could manage, Jadin walked up to him, ignoring the beautiful bouquet of red roses he offered. At six foot three, Landon towered over her. "What exactly did you hope to gain by coming here? We both agreed that the marriage was a mistake, which is why we had it dissolved."

"That is precisely *why* I came," he responded. "Jadin, we're still married. The divorce never happened."

Landon appeared to be enjoying her struggle to capture her composure. "I don't believe you." She could feel the electric heat coursing through her as if his sensual energy was powering up hers.

*Not now,* she told herself. *I can't think of him in that way.*

Jadin took in his beautiful brown eyes, close-cropped hair, his perfectly etched lips and muscular frame in a grey suit. His smooth cocoa-tinted complexion was free of hair. She glanced down at his shoes…shiny, black leather ones, without a smudge of dirt or a blemish. She was close enough to smell the citrusy scent of his aftershave.

Landon gave a slight shrug. "It's the truth. I never signed the papers and I didn't file them."

"Did you ever receive a copy of the final divorce decree?" Jordin asked her sister.

Jadin searched her memory. "Now that I think about it…no, I didn't."

"How could you get married and not tell your family?" Eleanor wanted to know.

"I knew about it," Jordin confessed. "I didn't say anything, because it was over so quickly, and I didn't feel like it was my place to tell anyone."

Etienne's voice sounded like thunder in the silence. "How could you be so reckless, Jadin? What were you thinking?"

"Daddy, I was in love with Landon," Jadin responded. "That's why I married him, but then Giselle's husband was killed—seeing what she went through… I realized that I couldn't live with Landon's decision to be a Secret Service agent." She had witnessed the anguish her cousin suffered when her police officer husband was struck down in the line of duty. Giselle was so heartbroken with grief that Jadin had decided she did not ever want to experience that kind of pain.

"I can't believe this," her father uttered.

"I'm not the first person to elope." Jadin sent a sharp glare in Landon's direction. She couldn't believe he would ever do something like this to her. It was just plain mean.

"You're so much smarter than this," her mother countered.

"I'm sorry I didn't tell you. If Landon and I had stayed married—I never would've kept the marriage a secret."

"It would've been nice to know that my daughter was getting married, *period*."

Her mother's teary eyes caused a stir of emotion inside Jadin. "I'm sorry," she said.

"Now what are you going to do?" her father inquired. "You've been a married woman all this time and you've been living like you were single."

She knew he was referring to her relationship with Michael.

Jadin looked at Landon. "Why did you let me believe you would sign the divorce papers? I'm involved with someone—someone I care deeply about." Jadin paused for a moment, then said, "He asked me to marry him last night and I said yes. I was going to announce my engagement during dinner."

Eleanor slumped down into a nearby chair, shaking her head. Rochelle rushed to her side, murmuring words of comfort.

*This is such a mess.*

"Jadin, I don't take marriage lightly," Landon said, drawing her attention back to him. "We rushed into it, but I didn't want to end it in haste, as well. It's not like I didn't try to talk to you about my decision. I tried calling you several times, but you would never return any of my calls."

It was true. He had called her for months after she left, but Jadin thought it was best for her to disconnect from him completely. "You could've left that message on voice mail."

"No, I couldn't," he responded. "This was something we needed to discuss."

"We *did* discuss it, Landon."

"*You* discussed it, then ran off before I could have my say."

With a slight smile of defiance, Jadin pulled out her phone. "I'm calling Nevada."

Landon shrugged in nonchalance. "Why would I come all this way to lie to you?"

Ignoring his question, she found the number for the clerk of court and dialed.

Jadin swallowed hard, lifted her chin and boldly met Landon's gaze. There was no way she would let him get away with this farce. "I need to verify if you have a final decree of divorce on file for Landon and Jadin Trent..."

Blinking with bafflement, she hung up, saying, "There's no record of our divorce. They have no record of the petition ever being filed."

Jadin and Landon stared at each other across a sudden, ringing silence.

"Why now?" Jordin suddenly blurted. "Landon, why are you here?"

His face was full of strength and confidence. "I thought my intentions were very clear. I came for my wife."

"I've never been your wife—not really." Jadin experienced a gamut of perplexing emotions. Disconcerted, she crossed her arms and pointedly looked away. "I can't believe this is happening."

"South Carolina requires that a marriage be consummated," her father interjected. "I believe Nevada has the same laws."

"Our marriage was consummated," Landon responded. "There was no alcohol involved, no fraud or misrepresentation. Our marriage is valid."

Arms still folded across her chest, Jadin glared at him, but was surprised by the look of sympathy in his gaze.

"I know that you and your family need some time to adjust to the news... I'm going back to my hotel." He pulled out a card. "This has my cell number on it. Call me when you're ready to talk."

"Oh, you'll definitely be hearing from me," she responded, while struggling to keep an even, conciliatory tone.

Landon laid the flowers on the counter. "I'll see myself out."

"No, I'll walk you out," Etienne said. "We need to have a conversation, man-to-man."

"Jadin, girl, *you is married.*" Rochelle threw back her head and laughed. "He came all the way here to fetch his woman. All right, now... I like that."

"It's not funny, Aunt Rochelle. How am I going to tell Michael that I can't marry him because I already have a husband?"

"I don't know, but you better figure it out soon. I don't think Landon's going to wait too long."

"I have to agree with Rochelle," her mother said. "You need to talk to Michael right away."

"Why couldn't he just sign the papers?" Adding to Jadin's disappointment was a feeling of guilt.

"He doesn't want to end the marriage. That much is very clear." Jordin shook her head. "Landon's still in love with you."

"How do you feel about him?" Rochelle inquired.

"There is a reason you two got married in the first place. You are not one to take something like this lightly. Even though it was impulsive, you believed the two of you had a future together—I know you, Jadin. You wouldn't have married Landon otherwise."

"I care a great deal for Michael. We've been together for three years." In her mind, she was trying to figure out how she was going to explain this situation to him. When it came to Michael, there was no easy way—he was going to be angry regardless.

"But do you love him?" Eleanor asked.

Confused, she wandered restlessly around the room. "Who?"

"Michael. Do you love Michael?"

Jadin nodded.

"What about Landon?" Rochelle asked. "Are your feelings completely gone for him?"

There was no point in lying, so Jadin said, "I will always care about him, but that part of my life is over."

"He's got a marriage certificate that says otherwise," Eleanor said.

Jadin bit her lip to stifle the outcry. How could her life become messed up so quickly?

# Chapter 2

Landon moved to his mahogany desk in his hotel room and stared down at his reflection in its uncluttered surface. He considered how quickly his plan had fallen apart. He had been so certain that his strategy would work that he'd become over confident, overplayed his hand, which wasn't like him at all.

He had no idea that Jadin had never told her parents about the marriage. Had he known this, he would have taken a different approach. Landon wasn't sure which angered Jadin more—his not filing the divorce petition or the way he carelessly blurted out her secret to her family.

*I might have blown any chance I had of getting her back.*

He forced the thought out of his mind. He could not allow negative thoughts to take over. Landon was still in love with Jadin, which was why he moved to

Charleston instead of accepting his uncle Tim's invitation to come to Raleigh, North Carolina.

Not much about Jadin had changed since the last time he saw her five years ago. She still wore her warm brown hair in its naturally curly state, her smooth mocha complexion free of makeup and she still had an easy smile, although she did not spare him one. Not only was she beautiful, Jadin was very intelligent, as well.

Every time Landon thought of Jadin with the man she wanted to marry, his insides burned with jealousy and anger, despite his reasoning that she'd had no idea that she was still very much a married woman. Deep down, he had allowed himself to believe that Jadin had feelings for him still—that she would've been happy to see him once she got over the initial shock.

He was wrong, but Landon was not ready to give up just yet.

He had to come up with another plan to execute if he wanted to save his marriage. Landon vowed to do whatever he had to do to keep her from walking down the aisle with another man.

Jadin unlocked the door and walked inside. She had sat in the driveway for about fifteen minutes before pulling into the garage. She needed time to regain her composure. "Michael, are you here?" It was a useless question. Jadin knew he was home because his rental car was parked in the driveway.

He walked out of the kitchen, a glass of red wine in his hand. "Hey, babe. I didn't expect you back so soon. I figured you'd be eating with the whole DuGrandpre clan—you know how y'all do. I just finished eating. If you want, I can order something for you."

"I'm not hungry." Jadin sat down in the living room. She did not want to risk her knees buckling beneath her from the nervous energy running rampant through her body. She could not recall ever feeling so uneasy.

"Did you tell them about our engagement?"

She gave a tight smile and nodded.

Michael scanned her face. "What's wrong? What? They don't think I'm good enough for you? They *do* know my family has billions, right?"

He could be so irritating at times, she thought. "It's nothing like that, Michael. My family and I are not impressed by money."

"Then what is it?" He pointed to her left hand. "Where's the ring? Don't you like it?"

Jadin took it out of her pocket and placed it on her finger. "It's beautiful. I have to admit that I didn't think you would ever buy something this fancy."

"All it cost was six months' salary," Michael said as he sat down beside her. "I can't have my wife walking around with just anything on her finger. Once you move to Hollywood, we have a certain image to uphold."

"You know that you didn't need to spend that kind of money on me. Besides, I don't really need a ring to tell me that I'm married."

He looked at her as if she had grown two heads. "Are you *crazy*?" Michael ripped out the words impatiently. "Jadin, all the Alexander women have rocks on their hands. I can't have you walking around like I'm too cheap to get you something nice. I realize your family has accumulated a certain amount of wealth and status, but my family—we have billions. It's a whole 'nother level, I'm talking."

Jadin struggled not to lose patience with him. "Michael, *your* uncle Malcolm has billions. I read all about how he came into his money."

He retained his affability, but there was a distinct hardening of his eyes. "So, what are you trying to say?"

"I'm just saying that he didn't grow up with the trappings of wealth. Malcolm Alexander is one of the humblest men I've ever met. I don't think he'd care one way or the other if I had some huge ring on my finger or a simple gold band. Besides, rings are the last thing we need to be debating right now. We have much more to discuss." Awkwardly, Jadin cleared her throat. "Michael, there's something I need to tell you."

"What is it? What's going on?" She stirred uneasily in her chair.

"When I was in law school, I was involved with someone—well, right after we graduated, we went to Las Vegas to celebrate… He and I got married."

Complete surprise registered in his expression. "You were married?"

"Yes," Jadin responded. "I never mentioned it because it didn't last long. He and I went our separate ways."

A suggestion of annoyance hovered in Michael's eyes. "I appreciate you telling me… I'm just not sure why you waited until now to say something. Although I can't imagine you doing something so stupid."

Her back stiffened at his words. "It was *impulsive*, I admit. Something like this would have come out when we applied for a marriage license. That is one of the questions they ask. But just so you know… My own parents didn't know about this, either. Only Jordin. The thing is…I just found out my divorce was never finalized."

For a moment, Michael studied her intently. "What are you telling me? That you're still married? You're saying that I proposed to a married woman?" His vexation was evident.

Teary-eyed, Jadin nodded. "Landon's here in Charleston. He showed up at my parents' house earlier to inform me that he never signed the papers." She was irritated at the transparency of her emotions.

For an instant, Michael's gaze sharpened. "You're a lawyer," he uttered. "Jadin, how could you not know about this? I would think something like this would have been a priority. You could have checked for yourself. It's all public record."

"I trusted Landon to file the petition like he said he would. I wasn't worried, because I hadn't heard from this man in years. I know this was careless on my part, Michael. I promise I can get this straightened out long before we get married." She reached for him, but he moved away from her.

Michael got up and walked over to the mantel above the fireplace. He picked up the frame holding a photo of the two of them. "I'm so glad I didn't tell anyone I was proposing. Do you know how this is gonna look to my family? To my friends?" He paused for a moment, then asked, "Why did he come all the way here to tell you? Did he suddenly get an attack of conscience?"

"I refused to take any of his calls after I left him," Jadin said. "I never considered that the reason he was reaching out was to tell me that he'd decided not to sign the papers. Michael, I can fix this."

"I'm sure your family is very happy about this. You know they never wanted you with me."

"How can you say that, Michael?" Jadin asked. "They have been nothing but nice to you. You're the one who never wants to be around them."

He shrugged off her words. "I don't care to be around my own family."

"Then why did you go to your uncle and ask for a job?"

"Because I knew he'd give me something that came with a nice title and a salary to match."

"So, you used your uncle," Jadin said. "Because that's what it sounds like to me."

"He was a resource," Michael stated. "But this isn't about me. You messed up and now I need to straighten it out. I want to meet this man."

His words caught Jadin off guard. "Why?" she asked.

"I want to know what he's after," Michael said. "I don't believe he just came here to tell you that you're still a married woman. He could've sent you a letter or an email. This dude wants something, and I intend to find out exactly what it is."

"Michael, I'm sorry."

"This is not how I saw this night ending," he responded. "I think I'm going to sleep in the guest room."

Jadin wiped away her tears. Michael's disenchantment with her was written all over his face. She'd had no idea how he was going to react to the news, but she thought he would be more sympathetic to her plight. Instead, he was pulling away from her.

"Michael, I—"

He cut her off by saying, "I need some time alone to digest this news. I'll see you in the morning."

Jadin drew back as if she had been slapped. "As upsetting as this may be to you, there's no need for you to be rude, Michael."

"My apologies."

"Good night."

Jadin stayed in that one spot on the sofa until well past midnight. She had hoped Michael would return, offering a shoulder of support, but he did not.

She wiped away her tears, then made her way to her bedroom. Jadin paused outside of the guest room. She was tempted to knock on the door, but common sense overruled her heart. It was a struggle for him to fall asleep, so he often took a sleeping pill—the last thing she wanted to do was wake Michael, because she did not want to incur more of his ire.

Jadin entered her bedroom and removed her clothes.

She slipped on an old T-shirt and a pair of pajama pants, then climbed into her empty king-size bed.

Jadin's troubles kept her awake most of the night. She had not expected Michael to say that he wanted to meet with Landon.

*Nothing good will come out of that meeting.*

"I know," she whispered in the darkness. *I might as well brace myself for the inevitable.*

The next day, Landon could not wait to open the door to his hotel suite as he slid the key card through the door lock.

He was finally able to get away from the politics of work. The sunlight beamed into his hotel suite as the drapes opened to the ocean view.

Perfect. Breathtaking. This was the break he needed, but he could only savor it for a few minutes.

Today was his first day as deputy prosecutor, and it had been a bit overwhelming. It was expected of Landon to just dive right in.

*Nothing like on-the-job training.*

He spent the week prior in a series of workshops centered on his new role.

After changing into a pair of basketball shorts and a T-shirt, Landon checked in with his uncle.

"I was 'bout to call you, son," Tim Trent said. "How did things go between you and Jadin?"

"Not as I expected, Uncle. She never told her parents about the marriage—I hadn't considered that, as close as they are. Needless, to say...Jadin wasn't too happy with me coming to the house and announcing that I'm her husband."

"So, what's the plan now?"

"I'm giving her some time to adjust to the news. At least Jadin won't be rushing off to get married anytime soon."

"Do you really want her back if she's in love with another man?"

"No, Uncle... I saw them together, and while she seemed happy...there was something else. There were times I caught sight of a shadow of sadness or something. He would say something and then her whole expression would change. She'd try to cover it up with a smile or a nod, but it was there."

"So, how did you two leave things?"

"I gave her one of my old cards and told her to give me a call. I know that she's going to need a day or two to process all of this."

"I gather she doesn't know you're the new deputy prosecutor."

"Not yet. The official announcement will go out this week."

"I hope this pays off in the end for you, son. I advised you to pay Jadin a visit years ago, when she cut off all communication with you."

"I know, Uncle Tim… I admit that I held on to this because it was like the one card I could play when needed. The time came, and I played it. This was a gamble. I will either win or I'll lose."

"You know I want you to win. I'm praying for you and Jadin."

"Thank you. I need all the prayers you can send up. Jadin is the only woman I've ever loved, Uncle. I can't lose her."

They talked a few minutes more before getting off the phone.

His whole being seemed to be filled with waiting for something that might never come, but the call he had been expecting came an hour later.

"Landon, it's me," Jadin said.

There was a hint of apprehension in her tone. "It's good to hear from you. Are you ready to have that talk?"

"I am. Can we meet tomorrow night?"

"Sure. I'd like to take you to dinner," Landon said. "You can pick the place."

"My cousin Aubrie owns a restaurant. I'll text you the address."

"Thank you, Jadin."

"I'm not doing this for you, Landon. I'm doing it for me."

Although polite, Jadin was still upset with him—that much was clear in her voice, but he considered it a small victory that she was willing to meet with him. But it bothered him that her misery was like a steel weight.

More so because he was the cause of that misery.

# Chapter 3

As soon as they arrived at the restaurant, Jadin knew she needed to put some space between Michael and Landon. During the ride over, every time Michael looked at her, his eyes were large, glittering ovals of repudiation. Never once had he considered how she must be dealing with this—he only thought of himself and his humiliation.

When she saw Landon standing in the bar area, she walked up to him, saying, "I didn't tell you that Michael would be joining us because I didn't think you would come otherwise."

He surprised her by responding, "I'm fine with him being here. It's probably for the best anyway."

Jadin made the introductions.

Michael glared at Landon, who merely seemed amused.

"This is really awkward for all of us," she said.

Jadin forced herself to stay calm, although she was anything but. *Can this really be my life right now?*

A server arrived almost at once to take their drink orders.

When he left, Michael said, "When Jadin told me about the mistake she made with you, I decided I needed to meet you for myself. I want to hear from *you* why it took so long to tell her that the paperwork hadn't been filed."

Landon met his gaze straight on. "I don't make rash decisions on things like relationships and marriage. Michael, as much as I'm sure you don't want to hear this—the truth is that I still love Jadin and I don't want a divorce. *I never did.*"

"It wasn't your place to make the decision without me," Jadin interjected, her embarrassment turning to anger. "You had no right, Landon. Look at the position you've placed me in."

"You can't deny that I called you several times, but you never called me back. We jumped into this marriage impulsively—I didn't want to end it the same way and neither should you. The truth is that we never gave our marriage a real chance. You know that I'm right."

"Stop trying to play on her emotions," Michael snapped. "It's over between you and Jadin. She wants to be with me."

"I'd rather hear directly from Jadin what she wants and doesn't want," Landon responded. "She does have a mind of her own."

Jadin swallowed her trepidation. "We decided together that we'd made a mistake."

"No, we did not," Landon corrected her. "If *we* had,

the divorce would've happened. You did all the talking, handed me the papers and rushed out of the apartment."

"Jadin and I are going to get married," Michael interjected. "We can fly to Guam and get the divorce. All we have to do is spend at least seven days there before Jadin can file. The divorce will be final within a month or two. Then she and I can move forward with our wedding plans."

She noticed that Landon's expression did not change. He finished off his glass of water, then said, "Jadin won't do that. She's much more levelheaded. If she wants the divorce, it will be filed here in South Carolina. However, I thought I was very clear on my intentions." Landon met her gaze. "I want to give our marriage a real chance. We give it a year. If it does not work for either of us, I'll sign off on the divorce. Otherwise, the divorce will be contested."

"A *year*… You've got to be kidding me." Jadin settled back in her chair, disappointed. She could feel Michael's fury without looking at him. "On what grounds can you contest our divorce? We don't have children, money or property together."

"I'm sure I can think of a host of things. Infidelity, for one."

Jadin gave a sharp glare in his direction. "I thought I was a single woman."

Pushing away from the table, Michael uttered a string of profanity. "Let's get out of here before I hurt this dude. I can't take no more of his foolishness."

"Michael, you can leave anytime you want, but there's a lot more that Jadin and I have to discuss," Landon said. "Ultimately, this concerns the two of us. You have no say in what happens."

Michael glared at her. "Are you coming with me?"

"Landon's right," Jadin responded with a sigh. "We do have a lot to talk about."

Giving Michael a triumphant look, he said, "I'll see that she gets home safely."

Jadin could tell that Michael wanted to punch Landon in the face. She prayed it would not come to that, because if it did, her money was on Landon. Michael's bark was much worse than his bite. Landon had never been one to start a fight, but he would not back down from one, either.

Her body sagged with relief when her cousin Aubrie walked up to the table.

"Is everything okay?" she asked. "Looks like there's a whole lot of tension on this side of the room."

"I won't be staying for dinner," Michael said. "Jadin will be eating with her husband."

"Excuse me?"

Puzzled, Aubrie looked from Michael to Jadin, who said, "I'll tell you later."

She sat down in the chair Michael had just vacated. "No, I think I'd better hear this now."

Michael straightened his tie, then strode toward the exit doors with purpose.

Aubrie looked at Jadin. "Okay, so what the heck is going on?"

"Landon and I dated in law school. I'm sure you remember me talking about him."

She glanced over at him. "Yeah, I do."

"Remember you were supposed to come with us to Vegas, but you had to go to New Orleans for something...? I forget what."

"That's right," Aubrie murmured. "We were going

to celebrate your and Jordin's graduation from law school. I couldn't go because I was taking some classes at the New Orleans School of Cooking."

"The long and short of it is that Landon and I decided to get married while we were there."

Aubrie gave a short laugh. "That must have been some party."

Landon chuckled. "I've never touched a drink in my life. Jadin and I were in love."

"So, what happened between you two?" Aubrie wanted to know. "Why didn't you stay together?"

"I accepted a job with the Secret Service. My uncle worked with them for years. I lived for the stories he would tell, and so when the opportunity availed itself, I jumped. Jadin seemed fine with my decision at first, but then she decided that the marriage was a mistake."

"A couple of days after we got married, Giselle lost her husband in the line of duty," Jadin interjected. "I saw what it did to her and realized that kind of lifestyle wasn't for me. I gave him a signed petition for divorce. Landon led me to believe that he was going to sign and file it, but he never did."

"So, what happens now?" Aubrie inquired. "I have to say this is better than the book I'm reading right now."

"That's why I'm here," Landon stated. "I came to Charleston to get my wife back."

Aubrie stood up. "I think I'm going to leave you two to talk, then. Jadin, I'll call you tomorrow. We really need to have a conversation."

"I know."

When they were alone, Landon said, "You look beautiful, Jadin."

"I can't believe you did this to me. Look what delaying this information has caused. Now you're saying that you want us to give the marriage a year." Jadin shook her head. "I'm involved with another man."

"What *we* had together was really special. You don't think it's worth another shot?"

"I'm with Michael…"

Landon shrugged in nonchalance. "I'm sure you care for this man, but I don't believe that you love him—not the way that you loved me."

Her back stiffened and her chin rose up a notch. "That's presumptuous."

"Am I wrong?" he asked.

A vaguely sensuous jolt passed between them. It was so strong, Jadin needed a moment to gather her composure. "Landon, what we had is over. I want a divorce."

She detected a flash of pain in his gaze. Jadin didn't want to hurt him, but she also did not want to give him false hope.

"I'm not willing to give up that easily. Marriage is sacred."

"Michael's not going to go for this."

"Then is he the man you really want? He's not willing to wait a year for you? All I'm asking is that we give our marriage a solid try before throwing it out the window. After that, I'll give you the divorce—if it's what you truly want."

"Landon, how are we supposed to make a marriage work with you living in DC?"

"I live in Charleston now."

Jadin gasped in surprise. "When did this happen?"

"A couple of weeks ago."

"Are you working in the Mount Pleasant field office?"

He shook his head. "No, I left the Secret Service, Jadin. I'm deputy prosecutor."

"This a lot to deal with right now," she said.

"Then, let's just start with dinner," Landon suggested. "We can get reacquainted."

She glanced over her shoulder, half expecting Michael to be standing near the door, glaring at them. He was gone. Jadin picked up her purse and said, "Maybe I should go. He's pretty upset right now."

"Michael *chose* to leave. This is about you and me anyway. Right now, *our* marriage should be priority."

"Would you really divorce me on the grounds of infidelity?" Jadin asked.

"No, I would never do that to you. I didn't like Michael's cocky attitude."

She surveyed his face. "Why is this so important to you now?"

"It's always been important, Jadin. I don't know how many ways you want me to say this, but the fact is that I love you—you're my wife, and I want a real marriage with you."

He was serious. She could see the truth in his eyes.

"So, you returned to your law roots?" Jadin asked, changing the subject.

Landon nodded. "I knew that I would someday."

"I work in my family's law firm. I'm sure that doesn't come as a surprise to you. It's all Jordin and I talked about in law school."

"Until we got married." Landon shifted in his seat. "Then you were willing to walk away. When you left me, I figured it was because you were afraid of what your father would say—that and the fact that I wasn't willing to leave the Secret Service. If your cousin hadn't lost her husband in the manner that she did, you and I would still be together."

It bothered Jadin that Landon knew her so well. She wanted to show him that he did not know her as well as he thought. "I was going to move to California to be with Michael."

Landon looked surprised. "How did your father take the news?"

"He doesn't know," Jadin confessed. "I'd planned to tell him the day you showed up. Now he's dealing with the fact that I eloped and never said a word about it."

"I apologize for the way I handled this situation, Jadin. I really thought your parents knew about me— about us. The truth is that I panicked the night I saw Michael put that engagement ring on your finger. I was at the restaurant when he proposed. I had to move quicker than I'd planned."

"Oh, wow," she murmured. "Landon, this is such a mess."

"It's one that can be worked out."

Jadin glanced at him. "Hasn't there been anyone special in your life?"

"Not really," Landon said. "There was nothing long-term. I kept in the back of my mind that we were still married. I must admit that I always thought you'd come to your senses."

"Really?" She looked directly at him. "I figured you would never leave the Secret Service."

"And now?"

Jadin took a long sip of tea, hoping the nervous quivering in her stomach would stop.

Michael's ringtone went off, but she left it un-answered. She was not ready to deal with his bruised ego and temper tantrum at the moment. If she could have found a hole somewhere, Jadin would have gone running for it—this was a lot to deal with. Michael only made matters worse because he would find a way to make this situation all about him.

Landon watched the range of emotions on Jadin's face. "Do you really love Michael?"

After a moment, she responded, "I love him, but not in the way I loved you. He and I… We work."

Her honest response gave Landon hope. "You deserve more than that. Why won't you give our marriage a chance, Jadin? What we shared was real and it was special."

"I'm not sure I'm ready to do that. Landon, we've been apart for a long time. I know that I'm not the same girl I was back then—I'm sure you are not the same person, either. Most of all, I'm all over the place right now, so I don't want to make any decisions."

"Jadin, I didn't come here to hurt you or ruin your life," Landon said. "I came here because I believe you still love me as much as I love you. Because of the love we shared, we owe it to ourselves to try to see if our marriage is workable."

"This is just too much." Jadin pushed away from the table. "I need to go home and talk to Michael. That's if he's not already on a plane back to California."

"I'm not going to pressure you into staying with me. I just want you to take some time and think about my request. If you decide that it's really Michael who you want to be with, then I'll let you go. I promise."

"I'll think about it, Landon. I guess I owe you that much."

He pushed away from the table. "I'll drive you home."

"No, I'll take an Uber," Jadin insisted. "It's just better this way."

Sudden anger lit his eyes. "Are you afraid of him?"

"Landon…no, of course not. I wouldn't be with a man like that. Things are tense between us right now, as I'm sure you already know. I would rather just keep you two away from each other."

"You're sure?"

"You don't have to worry about me."

Michael was on the porch, waiting for her when she arrived.

"How could you humiliate me like that?" His voice rose with each word.

Jadin reacted angrily to the challenge in his voice by removing her Taser from her purse. "I know you're upset right now, but I'm telling you that you'd better go walk it off… Do whatever you have to do, but you will not come to my home and disrespect me like this."

He looked at the device in her hand. "You know I'd never put my hands on you."

"And you won't talk to me any kind of way, either." She permitted herself a withering stare to show she meant business.

"I apologize for raising my voice like that. It's just that this whole situation…"

"Don't you think I *know*, Michael? I know how upsetting this is for you and I'm sorry."

"So, how did you leave it with him?"

"He asked me to take some time and think about working on our marriage. He said if I decided that I would rather be with you, then he would give me the divorce."

"So, it's over, then?" Michael asked. "I wish I could've seen the look on that arrogant face of his." He chuckled. "I should've—"

Jadin interrupted him by saying, "I haven't given him an answer yet."

"What? What's wrong with you?" Curses fell from his mouth.

"You can leave," Jadin said, pushing past him.

Michael grabbed her hand. "Babe, I don't understand. I thought you wanted to be with me."

"I told Landon that I would think about everything and I intend to keep my word. This is a man who was once very important to me. I owe him that much."

"And what do you owe me?" Michael asked.

Jadin looked him straight in the face. "I owe you the truth and that's what I've given you."

"You also owe me that expensive engagement ring back."

She removed it from her finger and handed it to him. "Here you go."

"If you really loved me like you say you do, you would've told Landon to go straight to hell." A sudden chill hung on the edge of his words.

"I think that it's best you stay at the Alexander-DePaul hotel or wherever you want to go, but you can't stay here. I can't deal with your attitude right now."

"I'm sure you'd rather spend your time reliving your college romance with Landon." It was obvious he did not care whether he hurt her or not.

"That's really mature, Michael." Jadin walked into her house, slammed the door shut and locked it. "Jerk…"

* * *

"She brought Michael with her," Landon said when his uncle answered the phone. "You called it."

"No punches were thrown?"

"He wanted to," Landon responded with a chuckle. "Having met him now, I can tell you that I don't like him. He's definitely not right for Jadin." He picked up a pen and begin scribbling. "I really feel bad for her. I hate putting her in this position, but I don't have any other choice."

"So, where do you and Jadin stand?"

"I asked her to think about my proposal."

"Good. I'm glad you didn't pressure her into giving you an answer right now," Tim said.

"If Michael is the kind of man I believe he is, I don't have a thing to worry about. I can't see Jadin wanting to be with someone like him."

"Maybe she's no longer the woman you knew and loved."

"Why do you say that, Uncle?"

"She has been involved with this man and she did accept his proposal."

Landon's thoughts were suddenly disquieting. He swallowed hard, trying to manage a response. "I guess I hadn't really considered that."

"Son, all you can do now is wait. The ball is in Jadin's court."

"I'll let you know what happens," Landon said before ending the call.

He changed into a pair of sweatpants and a T-shirt. He needed an outlet to release some of the stress he was feeling. A quick workout was the answer.

All this waiting was torment, but he had no choice.

* * *

Not paying attention to where she was walking, Jadin bumped into her cousin Ryker at the courthouse the next day.

"Hey, what's going on?" he asked. "You look so distracted. I don't think you even saw me just now."

"Nothing much…except that my life is in shambles," she responded dryly. "Then Judge Tinsdale is in a bad mood. It's hot outside… You might want to stop me now because I can go on complaining."

Ryker checked his watch. "I'm taking you to lunch, Jadin. I've never seen you like this."

"I'm warning you now—you don't know what you're getting into, but I'm not going to turn down a meal. I didn't have breakfast this morning and I'm starving."

"My car or yours?"

"We can walk to Montell's, if you don't mind," she suggested. "I'm in the mood for shrimp and grits."

"That's fine. Where I'm parked is on the way, so we can put our stuff in the car."

She embraced him. "Thanks, cousin. I really appreciate this."

"Tell me what's going on with you."

"Michael asked me to marry him and I accepted—"

"Congratulations," Ryker interjected.

"Yesterday, when I went to tell my parents, things went in a direction I never expected."

He gave her a sidelong glance. "What happened?"

"My husband showed up. I'm really surprised your mother hadn't mentioned it."

Ryker stopped in his tracks. *"Your what?"*

"Yep. I have a husband and a fiancé. Well, I *had* a fiancé." She grabbed his arm. "C'mon, we're almost there. You're going to need to sit down while I pour out all the sordid details of this mess I'm in."

"I think I'm gonna need a drink, too."

"I *know* I need one," Jadin said, "but we're going to have to settle for the nonalcoholic version. Come by my place later tonight and we can really tie one on together."

As soon as they were seated in a booth beside a huge picture window, Ryker said, "Lay it on me. I need the whole story."

She waited until they had given the server their drink and menu selections.

"My husband's name is Landon Trent. We dated in law school. To celebrate our graduation, we went to Las Vegas. He accepted a job with the Secret Service and I was offered a job with a large DC law firm. We decided to get married and we did."

"Wasn't Jordin with you in Vegas?"

Jadin nodded. "She knew about the marriage. Anyway, we ended up cutting our vacation short because Aunt Rachel called to tell us about Chad's death. Jordin and I took the first flight we could get to be with Giselle."

"That's right," Ryker said. "I picked you up from the airport." He shook his head. "Giselle hasn't been the same since Chad died."

"Seeing her so grief stricken… It made me realize that Landon's job as a Secret Service agent would place him in some of the same scenarios as Chad. He was putting his life on the line daily and I just couldn't live with that. After the funeral, I went back to DC and told Landon that the marriage was a mistake."

The server arrived with their meals.

After blessing the food, Ryker sliced into his wood-grilled salmon. "Why didn't you get a divorce, if that was the case?"

"Now, this is where everything gets crazy," Jadin said. "I gave him a signed copy of the petition. I thought Landon agreed that ending the marriage was the right thing to do. I loved him so much, Ryker, and it broke my heart." Jadin stuck a forkful of shrimp into her mouth and chewed. She swallowed, then said, "We both sat there, tears running down our faces… I had to get out of there. I told him I was going home. I told Landon to take care of everything." The memory of that day still evoked a sharp pain in her heart.

"I'm guessing Landon never signed the papers."

"Once I came home, I dived straight into my work. I was in the attorney training program and you know how demanding Uncle Jacques can be—he was the instructor at the time."

Ryker nodded in understanding. "Yeah, my dad has very high expectations. He was a good teacher."

Jadin agreed. "I was so focused on living up to the DuGrandpre name and forcing Landon out of my heart… I just didn't think about the divorce anymore. In Nevada, it only takes three or four days for an uncontested divorce to be finalized. I trusted Landon to do his part and I thought we were good."

"Does Michael know?"

"Yes, I told him the same day I found out. Ryker, he was so hurt, but then he wanted to meet with Landon."

"I can understand that."

"The three of us had dinner last night. Well, Landon and I had dinner. Michael left."

"What happened?"

"Landon declared his love for me and said the reason he came to town was because he wants us to give the marriage a *year*. You know that conversation went left real quick."

"You've been married all this time," Ryker said. "What does he expect to change?"

"Oh, let me clarify. Landon wants us to live as man and wife for a year. He says we never gave the marriage a real chance."

"From what I'm hearing, he's right."

Jadin sent a sharp glare in his direction.

"I'm just saying."

"Michael was livid. He asked for his ring back, which I can understand. He flew out first thing this morning." Jadin did not add how Michael kept harping on his humiliation. How he was going to look like an idiot. He did not seem to care that she felt bad about the situation and had apologized.

"Why? Is it because you are considering Landon's proposition?"

Ryker's question pulled Jadin out of her reverie.

"Michael doesn't want to see me until I get my situation resolved, as he put it. The truth is that I don't know what to do, Ryker."

"Do you still have feelings for Landon? Because if you didn't, I don't think you would be this conflicted. You and Landon haven't lived as husband and wife… You know, if you really wanted to divorce him, you could just do it."

Jadin did not respond.

Ryker finished off his iced water. "This is what I think you should do. Take a couple of days off and go away somewhere, away from everybody to really sort out your feelings for both Landon and Michael. Your feelings for Landon were strong enough for you to go against all reason to be with the man you loved."

"You sound like your mother. Aunt Rochelle told me the same thing." Jadin wiped her mouth with her napkin. "To complicate things further, Landon moved here and is the new deputy prosecutor."

"Apparently, he's still in love with you."

"That doesn't make him the right man for me."

"Why do you say that?"

"I've moved on, Ryker. I've been living my life as a single woman for five years. He should've told me that we weren't divorced."

"You're angry with him."

"Yes, I am," Jadin admitted. "It makes me look bad. I can only imagine what people will say if it comes out. I'm an attorney and I had no clue that I was still married. How do I explain having a husband?"

"Since when did you start caring what others think?"

"Who is going to have confidence in me as an attorney? I didn't even verify my own divorce."

"First things first, Jadin. Decide if you're even going to stay in the marriage. Once you decide that, then we can tackle the rest."

"Thank you for not treating me like an idiot."

"Uncle Etienne got on you pretty good, huh?"

"Michael has probably been my worst critic, but I know that it's coming from a place of hurt. Dad hasn't really said much, but my mom. She is very upset. Ryker, I don't think Mom has ever been this angry with me."

"I'm sure it's more that she's disappointed."

She took a sip of her iced tea. "I still haven't told Austin."

"You'd better do it before my mother does," Ryker recommended. "How did she find out?"

"She was at the house when Landon came to ruin my life."

"I know you're not happy about this, but it's actually a good thing. What if you had gotten married to Michael without knowing? You'd have an even bigger problem."

"I guess you're right," Jadin said. "I can't even imagine how my mom would've handled that."

They finished their lunch, then headed back to the fourth-floor law firm on Broad Street, in the bustling downtown business district. Jadin glanced up at the portrait of Marcelle DuGrandpre, their grandfather. During a time of racial tension, Marcelle opened the doors of the DuGrandpre Law Firm in 1960. She felt a thread of shame as she eyed the picture. She missed her grandfather but was relieved he had not lived long enough to see this mess she'd created for herself.

Jacques DuGrandpre was waiting outside Ryker's office when they arrived, prompting him to ask, "Dad, do you need to see me?"

"I wanted to discuss the details of the Brylan case with you."

Jadin glanced up at the tall man, who was her uncle. "I guess you know what's going on in my life."

He nodded. "How you holding up?"

"I think I'm going to take Ryker's suggestion and go away for a few days. I have a lot to think about."

"I hear this man is our new deputy prosecutor," Jacques said. "Looks to me like he's come here to stay."

She gave a slight nod.

Her uncle followed Ryker into his office.

Jadin walked into the next office, closing the door behind her. She checked her calendar.

"Good," she whispered. "I can take the rest of this week off." She would drive down to Jekyll Island, Georgia. It was a perfect and peaceful setting for Jadin to ponder Landon's request.

She could not deny the mixed emotions she'd been experiencing since he sent her engagement to a crashing halt.

Jadin picked up the phone and dialed.

When she heard her brother pick up, she asked, "Are you busy? I need to talk to you. It won't take long."

Austin stood in her office five minutes later. "What's up?"

"I need to tell you something."

"Are you okay?" he inquired as he closed her door to give them some privacy.

"I am... Well, I'm not. Austin, I have a husband."

His surprise was evident, but he did not seem particularly thrilled. "You and Michael got married?"

"No, we didn't," Jadin responded. "I got married a few days after I graduated law school. My husband's name is Landon Trent."

"Wait... I'm confused. I thought you wanted to marry Mi—"

She cut him off by saying, "I thought I was divorced. Turns out that Landon never signed the divorce papers. I'm still a married woman."

"I don't know what to say."

"I'm just as shocked as you are, Austin. Trust me, I

never saw this coming. The sad thing is that Michael did ask me to marry him."

"How is he taking all this?"

"Not well at all."

"Well, you just have to wait until the divorce is final. Then you and Michael can start your life together, if that's what you truly want."

Shaking her head, Jadin said, "It's not that simple. Landon wants us to give our marriage a real shot before we call it quits. He's asked for a year to determine if we're meant to be together." Deep down, she could not stop herself from pondering the same thing.

"Man…"

"I can't believe this is my life right now."

"What do you want to do, sis?"

"I don't know. Michael wants nothing to do with me until the divorce is final. Landon wants to stay married."

"I'll ask you a second time. What is it that *you* want?"

"I really don't know, Austin. I'm leaving town tomorrow. I need to get away for a few days to think about my next move. I wanted you to know what's going on."

"I know everything looks crazy right now, but it's going to work out, Jadin."

Etienne opened the door and stuck his head inside. "Just heard from your sister. The doctor's placed her on bed rest for the rest of her pregnancy."

"What happened?"

Her father strode all the way inside. "She was experiencing some preterm labor. The doctor wants her to take it easy. Rochelle is going to take over Jordin's upcoming court cases for the next month. Austin, can you take the ones for the next month?"

"Yes."

"After that, Jordin will work from home until the babies are four months old."

"Dad, I'm taking the rest of the week off," Jadin announced. "There's nothing pressing on my calendar until Monday. If something comes up, Mindy is familiar with all of my cases." She had every confidence in her paralegal.

"I'll cover for Jadin if anything does come up," Austin said.

Etienne nodded. "I think it's a good idea for you to take this time off. I'll let your mother know."

After her father and Austin left, Jadin called her sister.

"Hey, how are you feeling?" she asked when Jordin answered the phone.

"I'm fine. The contractions have stopped for now. My doctor wants me to make it to thirty-two weeks before I deliver."

"Hopefully, the babies won't decide to make their entrance this weekend, because I'm leaving town for a few days. I need to get some clarity on my situation."

"Have you talked to Landon since y'all had dinner?"

"No. I don't want to talk to him until I've made a decision."

"Jadin, I know you love Michael, but I have to say that you and Landon had something special. He was your best friend. I don't see it between you and Michael. The other thing I notice is that your eyes don't light up the way they used to with Landon."

"Like I said, I have a lot to ponder."

"Have you even thought about Landon over the years?"

"You know I have," Jadin said. "I just didn't talk about him. The truth is that, as much as I've tried, I have never been able to get him out of my mind. People always say that you never get over your first love—I just figured this was the reason I couldn't stop thinking about him."

"Where are you going?"

"Jekyll Island."

"Oh, I wish I could go with you," Jordin said. "I love it there."

"Make sure you do as the doctor instructed. I'll call you as soon as I get back." Jadin ended the call.

Despite her busy schedule, thoughts of Landon intruded into her day. Seeing him again threatened to rekindle old forgotten feelings. For the moment, Jadin was trapped in the memory of her own emotions.

# *Chapter 4*

The warmth of the May sunlight kissed Jadin's skin as she walked from her car to the entrance of the Jekyll Island Club Resort, enjoying the greenery of the tall trees. She inhaled the freshness of the Atlantic Ocean. She gently held her hat as the cool island breeze swirled around her.

Jadin checked in at the lobby and was given her swipe key card.

The porter brought her baggage up and she gave him a generous tip, for which he was grateful.

"Finally," she whispered to herself with an appreciative grin as she entered her suite.

The clubhouse suite had a fresh sea scent to it. The sun beamed brightly as it welcomed Jadin in, the island breeze blowing gently as the blinds cackled against each other. She was all too glad to unzip her purple suitcase and pull out the summer dress she would wear later.

Jadin undressed and got into the shower.

The last time Jadin visited the island, Michael had come with her. They had explored the forest and sandy beach on horseback, although he'd complained the entire time. It was during their picnic lunch that she had gone full Nicholas Sparks on him.

Framing Michael's face in her hands, she'd told him, "I really think that you are my soul mate."

He'd laughed.

Michael's disbelief in soul mates was not really news to Jadin. Prior to that moment, they'd had a few discussions on the topic and had jointly categorized romantic destiny as a myth. The truth was that she and Michael had never been a perfect fit.

Jadin could not deny that she'd had to modify her idea of Mr. Right. Despite being tall, dark and handsome, Michael approached the world differently from her. He was more carefree, less detail oriented. The more she thought about it, Jadin recognized that, even in its healthiest form, their relationship was less than what she considered perfect.

"Our relationship doesn't require the fairy tale of *happily-ever-after*," she whispered. Michael was limited in his ability to enrich her spirit.

Landon was different. With him, Jadin felt safe enough to let her truest self out. He made her feel whole, with no piece missing from the puzzle. Her relationship with Landon had been more intense than her relationship with Michael, in both good and bad ways.

"What am I doing?" she asked the empty suite. "Michael is a good man and he loves me."

*Do you love him?*

Stunned, Jadin wondered where that question could have come from. *Of course, I love him. I love Michael.*

*Then why are you here?*

She had no answer for that question.

From all she knew and had read, Jadin knew that soul mates were connected on a deeper level and were willing to take on the world as long as they were together. She knew that soul mates were mentally inseparable— despite being apart, they were always in tune with one another.

Just in the brief time Landon had come back into her life, she felt he knew and understood her more than Michael ever could. He was willing to give her the time she needed to sort this out, while Michael wanted her to make a quick decision and be done with the entire matter. He didn't seem to understand why she would even consider Landon's request.

Jadin did not want to hurt either man, but more than that, she did not want to make a rash decision that she might end up regretting for the rest of her life. She owed it to herself to consider both possibilities.

The next morning, she walked along the surf with flip-flops in hand, enjoying the island breeze swirling around her.

Jadin eyed the couple just ahead of her, who were obviously smitten with each other. They walked hand in hand, laughing and talking. Every now and then, they would stop and pick up seashells. She loved everything about Jekyll Island. The beaches, saltwater marshes and oaks draped in Spanish moss. The awesome beauty of the island was the reason she brought Michael here, but he did not share her appreciation for the landscape and historical landmarks that were prevalent on the island.

Unlike Michael, Jadin knew that Landon would enjoy visiting Jekyll. They had traveled most of the Underground Railroad route from Virginia to Canada. They vowed one day that they would go down to Georgia and explore the route from there to Virginia. After they broke up, Jadin did not want to complete the journey without him.

Landon's thoughts turned to Jadin. He had not heard from her since the night they had dinner. He wondered if she remembered that Monday would be their fifth wedding anniversary. He vowed to himself that he would give her whatever space she needed, and Landon intended to keep that promise.

The receptionist called to let him know he had a visitor.

Landon checked his calendar. "I don't have any appointments. Who is it?"

"Austin DuGrandpre."

Landon vaguely recalled Jadin mentioning she had an older brother by that name. "Send him back."

He got up and walked out of his office to meet Austin.

"C'mon in," Landon said. He closed the door to give them some privacy.

"I came here to decide if I should welcome you to the family."

"Straight to the point," Landon responded. "I like that."

"I want to know what your end game is," Austin stated. He leaned back in the chair and folded his arms across his chest.

"I want my wife," he responded. "That's it."

"And if she doesn't want to be with you? What then?"

"Jadin just has to tell me, Austin. I'm not going to force her to stay in this marriage any longer. She has to want to be with me—if she doesn't, I'll give her what she wants."

"But you don't believe she wants a divorce. Is that it?"

"I'm sure she thinks she does, but we've been apart for all this time. Austin, I can't explain it to you, but what Jadin and I have is special. She admitted to me that she doesn't love Michael in the same way that she loved me. I saw them together the night he proposed." Landon paused for a moment, then said, "She didn't look all that happy with him. I'm pretty sure I don't have to tell you that—you've seen it yourself."

"I want what's best for my sister," Austin said. "But right now, I can't really say that you are what's best for her."

"Yet, you know Michael is not the right man for her. I can see it in your face."

"This is Jadin's decision," Austin said. "Let her make it without any manipulation or games on your part."

"Your sister's too smart for games. I would never insult her in that manner."

"Look me in my face and tell me that you love Jadin."

"I love your sister with every part of my being, Austin. I have never loved another woman—it has always been Jadin."

An expression of satisfaction showed in his eyes.

Standing up, Austin said, "It's nice meeting you. I have a feeling I'll be seeing a lot of you and not just in court."

"I hope that you're right."

Landon walked Austin out to the lobby.

"Remember what I said. No games or manipulation. Let Jadin make up her own mind."

"I give you my word."

Landon headed back to his office.

"I see you're meeting the family," his boss said from the doorway. "No black eye or broken bones. I guess things must be going okay."

"As well as can be expected for now."

Deep down, Landon prayed Jadin would agree to making their marriage a real one, but he knew that if Jadin really did not want to stay in the marriage, there was nothing he could do but accept her decision.

Landon knew that he wasn't made to live alone, without being surrounded by family, and being with Jadin was *right*. He was not afraid of taking risks, but this time felt different. The stakes were higher, and he admitted something to himself—something he would never have disclosed to another living soul, not even his uncle.

He was scared.

Back at home, Jadin unpacked and did a couple of loads of laundry. When she'd left Jekyll Island that morning, she knew what she needed to do. However, Jadin was not ready to share her decision with anyone, not even Landon. Part of her wanted to punish him a little. She was not going to make it that easy for him.

Jadin turned on the television.

"Millicent Witherspoon-Herndon was discovered

in her bedroom, covered in blood, by the maid…" the reporter was saying. "Mrs. Witherspoon-Herndon was a prominent figure in Charleston's social landscape…"

Jadin shook her head. "Another senseless murder."

She strolled into the kitchen and pulled a tomato and an onion from the fridge. The eggs she'd boiled an hour ago sat on the stove.

"…her husband, Blaine Herndon, was at home at the time of the attack. Investigators refuse to confirm whether the wealthy real estate developer is a person of interest…"

Jadin opened a can of tuna. She chopped up the eggs and onion, placing them inside a bowl. She added the tuna, mayonnaise and sweet relish. She then carved out the inside of her tomato, replacing the contents with the tuna salad.

Fifteen minutes later, Jadin sat at the counter, eating while she watched the rest of the news.

Her thoughts strayed to Landon. She had put off contacting him long enough. Jadin had made her decision before leaving the island, but she did not want to tell him over the phone.

After she finished eating, Jadin cleaned up her kitchen. She glanced over at the clock on the wall. "Time to get this over with," she murmured.

Landon answered on the second ring.

"Hey, it's me."

"I'm really glad to hear from you."

"Are you busy tomorrow evening?" Jadin asked, keeping all emotion out of her tone.

"No. No, I'm free."

"Great, because I'm ready to discuss what happens next. I'll text you my address. Is seven good for you?"

"It's fine."

"Thank you, Landon. I'll see you then."

Jadin walked over to the fireplace and picked up the photo of her and Michael. She had not heard from him since he left Charleston. She stuck it into the cardboard box on the floor.

# Chapter 5

Landon reread the text message that Jadin had sent after their conversation last night. She was true to her word, only sending him the address. Landon had thought it best not to mention that he already knew where she lived—it might make matters worse.

"She's really not going to give me a hint as to what she's decided." Curiosity was getting the better of him and Landon was sure this was her intention. *Jadin wants to make me sweat a little. I guess I deserve it.*

Still, he could barely hold his joy. He had hoped but thought he would not hear from her for a week or two.

His phone began vibrating.

"Hey, Uncle," Landon greeted. "What are you up to?"

"I figured I'd check to see how you're doing with your *wife*."

"I heard from her last night. She invited me over to her place this evening. I don't know if it's to demand a divorce or what, but I know Jadin. She is not going to rush into anything without giving it a lot of thought. I just hope that her decision weighs in my favor."

"She rushed into a marriage with you."

"Not really, Uncle," Landon said. "We had been talking about getting married several months prior to graduation. It just felt right when we were in Vegas. That's why I proposed to her. Then that night, we decided to get married."

"Son, I'm proud of you for wanting to make your marriage work, but I have to tell you—this might not turn out the way you want. I really don't want to see you get hurt."

"I know," Landon responded. "Uncle, it's a risk I had to take. I love Jadin that much. She is truly the other half of me. As corny as that sounds, it's true."

"Well, I know you got to get to work, so I'll let you go."

After his shower, Landon turned up the volume on his television when the reporter began talking about the Witherspoon-Herndon murder. He had been at the police station yesterday when investigators brought in Blaine Herndon for questioning.

According to Blaine, he and Millicent were home alone. She complained of a headache and went upstairs to their bedroom. He decided to stay downstairs. He claimed that he had fallen asleep and did not awaken until he heard the housekeeper screaming. His eyes moved to the right, which could indicate that he was remembering the events of the night before. From his training, Landon knew that the eyes of suspects tended to move to the left if they were trying to think of an alibi. Not once had Herndon shown anything other than a calm demeanor.

Landon agreed with the police detectives that Herndon's emotions did not raise any suspicions. But he didn't appear to be a person who showed a lot of outward emotion. His response to every question appeared to be the truth, and while he showed a willingness to cooperate with the investigation, Landon's instincts told him that the man was hiding something.

He personally found the small soundproof interrogation room with nothing on the walls, three chairs and a desk claustrophobic, so it was interesting that Herndon had not lawyered up or displayed that get-me-out-of-here reaction at all during the questioning.

The police intended to hold Herndon for seventy-two hours until the prosecutor decided to charge him. Landon was given the case and intended to sign off on the arrest first thing in the morning, but he was more interested in the motive. They were a loving and happy couple, according to friends and family. Millicent's family had money, but Herndon was a billionaire, so he did not kill her for wealth.

Landon made a mental note to investigate Herndon's finances—to make sure he did not have any financial woes no one knew about. He also wanted to review any insurance policies on Millicent.

He turned the television off and sat there, looking out the window. *Why did I wait so long to come after her? Because I wanted Jadin to figure out on her own that we belonged together.*

Landon knew that Jadin had every right to be angry with him. It wasn't as if she had gone into hiding. He could have showed up at her parent's home or the law firm at any given time. He could have sent her a letter, telling her of his decision not to end their marriage.

The truth of the matter was that Landon was afraid to lose her. It wasn't right, but still he had held on to his legal claim as her husband.

*We belong together. I know it and somewhere, buried deep in her heart, Jadin knows it, too.*

Jadin rushed to her desk and turned on her computer. She wanted to check on some of her cases before the staff meeting.

Mindy knocked on her open door before strolling inside. "Good morning. I bought you a cup of tea."

Jadin smiled and accepted the mug. "Thank you."

The paralegal sat down in one of the visitor chairs facing her desk. "I knew you'd come rushing into this office, but there are no fires to put out. Mr. Sanford called on Thursday to see if you were able to get his case postponed. I confirmed that you did and gave him the new date."

"Didn't we mail him a letter with this information?"

Mindy nodded. "He said he hadn't gotten it yet."

"What about Teresa Holliday?" Jadin asked. "She usually calls every day."

"She called on both Thursday and Friday," Mindy confirmed. "I talked to her, and so did Austin. I think he was able to get through to her. He explained to her that we are doing everything we can to get her son's charges kicked down to juvenile court."

"I know she's really worried. She took out a second mortgage to pay for my services. Her son is not a bad kid. He made a huge mistake, but he shouldn't be tried as an adult. I have a meeting with the prosecutor tomorrow morning."

Jadin thought about Landon. She was grateful that he wasn't the prosecutor on this case. At this point, she was not ready to work with him—she needed to adjust to the idea that they were still husband and wife.

The last thing they needed was to have to face each other in court.

She returned a couple of phone calls, responded to emails and electronically filed a couple of documents before joining the other attorneys and paralegals in the large conference room.

Jadin took a seat across from Mindy.

"We just landed the Herndon case," Jacques announced when he blew through the door. "I just got off the phone with him."

"Blaine Herndon?" Jadin asked. "The man whose wife was brutally murdered in her bedroom. It's been all over the news."

Her uncle nodded. "Blaine's asked specifically that you represent him, Jadin. He said that you represented a friend of his in the past, and he was pleased with the way you handled yourself in the courtroom. He has every confidence that you are the right lawyer for him."

"Has he been arrested?" she asked.

"No, but he expects to be at any time. He's been in a holding cell since they took him in for questioning," Jacques responded. "He's pretty sure that the police aren't buying that he slept through the attack on his wife—he says it's the truth."

Jadin picked up her pen. "I'll meet with him as soon as possible."

"Landon Trent is the prosecutor reviewing the case," her father interjected.

She stopped writing. "Are you sure?"

He nodded.

"Then maybe Austin or Tracy should represent Blaine," Rochelle suggested. "There are some ethical considerations when a defense attorney and a prosecutor for the same county are married to one another."

Jadin could not believe that her aunt just put her on blast like that. Not everyone in the conference room had any knowledge of her marriage to Landon.

Mindy glanced at her in confusion.

She cleared her throat loudly, then said, "Some of you don't know this, but the new deputy prosecutor is my husband. We eloped after law school but separated not too long after. Recently, we've decided to reconcile…" Jadin could feel everyone's gaze on her. She forced herself to project an outward calm she did not have. She had not even told Landon yet that she was willing to give their marriage a chance. She had never felt so out of control where her own life was concerned.

"According to ethical guidelines, Jadin can represent a client being prosecuted by her prosecutor husband as long as there is disclosure of the marital relationship to the client and written consent is given. The prosecutor has to also give consent." Her father looked at her. "Just make sure you are vigilant in maintaining your client's confidences."

"That won't be a problem," Jadin stated.

After the meeting ended, she packed her tote and grabbed her keys. She needed to get to the jail to meet with Blaine Herndon.

Austin walked her outside to her car. "I take it that

you've made your decision based on what you said during the meeting."

She looked up at him. "I have. I'm going to give Landon what he wants. I'm going to give our marriage a real try."

"For what it's worth, I think you're doing the right thing."

"Really? Why is that? You haven't even met Landon yet."

"Actually, I have," Austin responded. "I went to see him."

Jadin put a hand to her face. "Oh, no…"

He chuckled. "Sis, nothing bad happened. I just wanted to make sure he wasn't gonna try to manipulate you into staying with him. My first impression of Landon is that he's honest and straightforward. One thing I'm absolutely sure of, and that is he really loves you, Jadin." Austin eyed her. "I have a feeling you still have some unresolved feelings for him, or you wouldn't have considered staying in this marriage."

"I don't know what it is about him, but I need to at least try to make this work. I feel like I owe it to Landon."

"You owe it to yourself, sis."

Landon pushed back his chair as police detectives Mike Solomon and Tracy Fielding walked out of his office. He had just signed off on charging Blaine Herndon with first-degree murder.

Millicent Witherspoon-Herndon had been stabbed ten times in what had to be a fit of rage. The knife used had been taken from the kitchen. Crime scene investigators had not found any bloody clothes belonging to her husband. They did find a damp bath towel with traces of blood on it in the laundry bin. Landon could not understand why Herndon got rid of his clothes, but not the towel.

Going over the evidence and Herndon's interrogation notes consumed the rest of Landon's day.

Shortly after 5:00 p.m., Landon walked across the parking lot to his car.

He had an hour in which to get home and freshen up before meeting up with Jadin.

"Lord, I really need this second chance with my wife," he whispered.

Landon also told himself that he would accept her decision no matter what it was. There was a chance that his heart would be ripped into shreds, but at least he could walk away knowing he had given it his best shot.

He recalled the moment he walked into her parents' house and coming face-to-face with Jadin. Their chemistry was electrifying. All he could think about at that time was that they were so perfect together.

Landon knew that it was going to be hard to accept if she wanted out of his life.

He believed that she had experienced that same jolt when their gazes met and held. Or maybe it was just his imagination. He sighed deeply.

Seven o'clock couldn't come fast enough for him.

# Chapter 6

Jadin looked down at the baggy sweatpants and T-shirt she was wearing. Landon was due to arrive at any moment.

*Maybe I should change clothes.*

She dismissed the thought as quickly as it had come. *Why am I worried about what he's going to think?* This was part of her normal routine. As soon as she arrived home, Jadin sought comfortable clothing.

The doorbell sounded.

Jadin opened the door. "I see you're still very prompt. I guess some things never change."

He smiled. "I see you still like your sweats."

"We can talk in the living room," she said.

He followed her.

Once they were seated, Jadin stated, "Landon, I thought about what you said, and I agree that we didn't really give the marriage a chance. I ran home to Charleston and never looked back, but in the back of my mind, I've always wondered if we could have worked." She held up her left hand. "Michael took back his engagement ring. Even if he hadn't, I would have given it to him."

"So, does this mean that you're giving us a chance?"

"It's not like I had a real choice in the matter."

"Jadin, I want you to be as fully committed as I am in this marriage. If you're not, then it's not going to work."

"Where are you staying?" she asked.

"The Mills House Hotel."

"If we're going to try to make this work, then I guess you might as well move in here with me. I have an extra bedroom—that's where you'll be sleeping."

"I'm fine with that for now," Landon replied. "At some point, though, that will need to change if we want to have a real marriage."

"Why did you really leave the Secret Service?" Jadin inquired, changing the subject. "I know you didn't just do it for me."

"There were several reasons," Landon said. "Most of it had to do with the many hours of unpaid overtime, the salary cap... I no longer saw the benefits. The other reason had to do with Uncle Tim. Did you hear about the attempt on Congressman Mitchell's life? It's been almost a year now."

"I read about it," she responded.

"My uncle was on his protection detail and he took two bullets...one in the leg and the other in his back. It was fortunate that no permanent damage was done, but it forced us both to examine what we wanted out of life. My uncle decided to retire. He finally got married a couple of months back. I realized that I wanted nothing more than to be with the woman I loved—*you*."

"I'm glad to hear that your uncle survived. I know how close you two are." She smiled. "Does he still make gumbo for you every Christmas?"

"He does," Landon responded. "I almost reached out to you when he got shot, but I figured it wasn't the *right* time."

"I don't know if there would have ever been a right time."

"You're probably correct," he said.

"What I don't like about this is that you manipulated me, Landon. This was a card you could play at any time," she said. "You could control my life."

"I wasn't trying to control you, Jadin."

"Really? Be honest, Landon. It thrills you that I had to walk away from the man I wanted to marry."

His eyes searched her own. "Is that what you really want? To marry Michael? Because if you do, then there's no point going through with a sham of a marriage. If you really want to be with Michael…"

"Landon, I'm choosing to give our marriage a chance. But I can't pretend that I haven't been involved with another man for three years." Jadin did not share that there were some things in her relationship with Michael that gave her pause. All he needed to know was that she was committed to working on her marriage.

"I don't want you to feel as if your hands are tied, Jadin."

"Despite the way this all came about, I made my decision of my own free will."

He relaxed visibly.

"Landon, there's something else you need to know.

I'm representing Blaine Herndon. I disclosed our relationship to him and he still wants me to be his lawyer."

*This is the last thing Jadin and I need—to be on opposite sides of the same case.* Marriage was for a lifetime. Or at least Landon intended it to be, but he wasn't so sure his already-fragile one could survive something like this. Both of their careers were at stake with such a high-profile case. "Can't you get it reassigned to one of the other attorneys in your firm?"

"I could, but why should I?" she asked. "Blaine Herndon specifically asked that I represent him."

Landon did not respond.

"Do you have a problem with this?"

"No…it's fine, Jadin."

She looked into his eyes and he hoped she saw the determination, the drive and steely ambition. He felt centered and focused. Goal oriented. Jadin had admitted to admiring those qualities about him. He had always been a hard worker and did not allow anything to distract him from his mission. "You want this case more than anything, don't you?"

"I do. It would be a high mark for my career as a prosecutor."

There had to be a way for them to do their jobs and still work on their marriage. For years, Landon had an intrinsic faith that things would work out in the end, so what he needed to do was stop worrying and act.

He reached inside his blazer and pulled out an envelope from the inside pocket.

Landon looked up to see that Jadin had one in her hand, as well.

They burst into laughter.

"I wasn't sure you remembered," he said.

"Just because I believed we were divorced, doesn't mean that I would ever forget the day we got married. Happy anniversary."

Landon smiled. "Happy anniversary."

He took this as a sign of better things to come.

The next day, Jadin left work early to prepare the guest room for Landon. He had checked out of the hotel earlier in the day. They were starting their life together as husband and wife.

It surprised her at how peaceful she felt in her decision. For some time after Landon left the night before, Jadin felt a warm glow. She clung to the memories of their time together in law school and of the day she married him.

The realization hit her that she never had experienced the same feelings with Michael, but then he was not a very romantic man. He would often say, "Romantic people believe in the ideal love they see on television. These types of people are obsessed with romantic movies, songs and finding their soul mates. That's not me. I think about love with my mind and my decision is based on logic. For example, you and I—we have common interests and you're beautiful… Our relationship can work."

Jadin was applying the finishing touch to the bed when a car door slammed. She could not see the vehicle, but a quiver along her spine told her it was Landon before she reached the door and peered outside.

Sure enough, he was skirting around the front of an SUV. Jadin pressed a hand to her heart, trying to calm the thumping there.

He was early.

She opened the door before he had time to knock.

They stared at each other. Long, muscled legs filled out faded jeans, and he wore a plain navy T-shirt that accentuated the broadness of his torso. Jadin didn't know what to say, and as the silence stretched out, she grew more and more uncomfortable. She chewed on her bottom lip, while Landon stood so still, she could barely make out the slight rise and fall of his chest as he breathed. It was like he was waiting to see what she would say before he decided what to do.

"Good evening." He smiled, but his eyes were focused on her lips, which she was still biting nervously.

"You're early." The words came out more sharply than Jadin had intended, but the fact of the matter was she was more affected by his appearance than she cared to admit.

His jaw ticked ever so slightly in response to her tone. "It's one of the qualities you used to appreciate about me."

"I still do," she responded. "Landon, I'm just a bit nervous about all this—you living here."

"I know we have to give it some time. But you should start to feel more comfortable around me before long."

"You sound really confident."

"That's because I am," Landon replied.

"I should give you a tour of the place."

He followed her from room to room.

"I guess we will have to share the office," Jadin said when she walked into the guest room, where he would be staying.

"I can put a desk in here," Landon said. "There's enough room."

They stood at the end of the queen-size bed. Jadin looked around. "Yeah, I guess you could."

"I have another box in the car." Landon left the room and went downstairs.

Jadin heard the front door open and close.

Minutes later, she heard Landon come back inside the house.

She walked out of the room in time to see Landon coming up the stairs. Jadin blew out a breath, wondering how they were going to survive the next twelve months.

They ordered pizza for dinner.

"Do you feel as awkward as I do?" she asked.

"Incredibly."

They burst into laughter.

The laugh had done much to dissolve the polite tension that had risen between them.

"Landon, I don't want you to feel out of place. I want you to feel like this is your home, too."

"I want that, too. More than anything, I want the life we should have had together."

Jadin pointed to the pizza. "You want another slice?"

"Sure." He smiled. "I see you remembered how I like it. Pepperoni, sausage, onions and black olives."

"How could I forget? You ate it for like three months straight our first year in law school."

Landon chuckled. "Hey, it was all I could afford." Giving her a sidelong glance, he asked, "Is that why you started inviting me over for dinner?"

"I knew that you couldn't survive on pizza alone." Jadin handed him a tiny box.

He opened it, revealing a key and a card.

"That's your key, the code to the alarm system and

the Wi-Fi password. I also have a garage opener for you, but it wouldn't fit in the box."

Landon kissed her on the cheek. "Thank you."

The smoldering flame she saw in his eyes drew her like a magnet and brought long-buried emotions to life. His nearness made her senses spin.

The evening was quiet, with only the fading sounds of birds echoing through the soft twilight. Landon had disappeared shortly after they had eaten, leaving for the gym.

Jadin sat outside and rocked gently in the porch swing, listening to the sounds of impending night and watching the moonrise off to her left. There was an owl somewhere close by, his call echoing plaintively as she caught sight of headlights approaching from the street.

He was back.

Jadin watched the garage door open as Landon pulled his car inside.

Minutes later, he appeared as she rocked the swing, sending it swaying gently back and forth.

"How was your workout?" Jadin asked.

"Grueling but good."

She smiled up at him, pointing. "There's an owl over there somewhere. I love the sounds of nature."

"I remember," Landon responded. "You were always wanting to go camping."

"You loved sleeping in the outdoors. Admit it."

He grinned. "I enjoyed it with you."

Landon sat down beside her, and they rocked in companionable silence as the night deepened.

It was a marvel how they could sit and not feel the need to speak. It was one of the things Jadin most enjoyed about his company. It was comfortable.

"My parents invited us over for dinner on Sunday. The whole family gets together, and it rotates from one house to the other. It's our thing."

"That's fine," Landon responded. "I'm looking forward to it. It'll give me a chance to redeem myself with your parents. I don't think I made a very good first impression."

"Just be prepared to be grilled about your entire life."

He laughed.

"I'm serious," Jadin stated. "They are going to want to know everything there is to know about you."

"Did they do this to the guy Jordin married?"

"They've known Ethan since he was eleven or twelve," she responded with a grin. "Are you scared?"

Landon shook his head no. "Nah...should I be?"

"I guess we'll see on Sunday." Jadin stopped swinging and rose to her feet. "I'm tired, so I'm going to call it a night. I'll see you in the morning." She paused in the doorway. "I usually grab some toast and a boiled egg for breakfast."

"I get up early enough to cook," Landon said. "I'll have something prepared for you by the time you're ready to leave."

"You don't have to do that."

"You're my wife. It will be my pleasure. Besides, you need to eat more than just an egg and toast."

Landon got up and walked to where she was standing. He turned to face her, his warm gaze delving into hers, drawing her in and making her thoughts drift away on the evening breeze. He planted a soft kiss on her lips, then said, "Good night."

Jadin stepped away from him. "Good night," she murmured.

Upstairs in her room, she still felt the warmth of his kiss. At least she imagined she could. After all this time, Landon still had a strong effect on her.

She felt a thread of guilt over the way her red blood cells had instantly responded to his kiss with the shocking eagerness of a young girl experiencing her first love. Their connection had short-circuited all the hormones she had placed in cold storage until she and Michael could be together.

One kiss from Landon, and they had instantly defrosted.

# *Chapter 7*

Landon punched his pillow with his fist. He was having a tough time sleeping, knowing that Jadin was just down the hall. Although she tried to keep her expression blank, he knew that their connection was still very much alive. He caught a glimpse of it in her eyes right before she walked away.

He knew that she believed her heart belonged to Michael, but Jadin was wrong. Landon was convinced that there was still a part of her heart that belonged only to him. Just in the brief time that he was in Michael's presence, he could tell that the man was all wrong for Jadin. In time, she would realize it, as well.

Landon had no doubt that Michael was a good man. He was just not the right one for Jadin.

*She is my wife. I should be in bed with her.*

He did not need excuses or reasons why he was so

determined to win Jadin back. It was clear. She was *his* wife and soul mate. They belonged together.

"I have to get my wife back," he whispered. "There is no me without her."

Landon lay on his side, listening to the heavy silence and wondering if Jadin was having as tough a time sleeping. His body hungered for hers, but it was too soon for intimacy. He was willing to wait until Jadin was ready, even if it killed him.

He finally gave up on sleep and got out of bed.

Landon left his room and went downstairs. On nights he could not sleep, he would make himself a cup of tea. He knew Jadin was a tea drinker as well, so he was sure he could find some in the kitchen.

Jadin was sitting in her office in front of her laptop when she heard Landon coming down the steps. She had not been able to sleep, so she decided that she could get a head start on her work.

She got up and opened her door tentatively.

He went into the kitchen.

"Landon?" she called out.

"Did I wake you?" he asked.

Jadin walked out to where he could see her. "No, I was actually down here, trying to get some work done."

"You can't sleep, either?" Landon opened the door to the pantry. "Is this where you keep the tea?"

"Yeah," she responded. "On the second shelf."

He glanced over his shoulder at her. "Do you normally have problems sleeping?"

Jadin sat down in one of the chairs at the counter and played with the vase of flowers in front of her. "No, not really. You?"

Landon shook his head no.

"Do you think it's because we're nervous?"

He grinned. "I'm not nervous, Jadin."

"Whatever…" she muttered. His presence gave her unexpected joy. It reminded her of the late nights they spent studying and writing legal briefs.

"I know this feels a bit strange," Landon said as he poured hot water into two cups. "If you want to know what's really keeping me up—"

"I do," Jadin quickly interjected.

"It's you. It's hard to sleep knowing that you—my wife—are sleeping just down the hall. You're so close, but there's still a gulf between us."

"I'm sorry," she said.

"Don't apologize, Jadin. None of this is your fault." Landon handed her a mug.

"Thanks."

"I don't want this transition to be uncomfortable for you." He took a sip of tea. "I'm going to only ask this one more time. Are you really sure about this, Jadin?"

"You wouldn't be here if I wasn't."

Jadin had always thought she would find her soul mate, be married and have children of her own by now. Maybe that was why she was so willing to settle down with Michael. She certainly did not want to be miserable in a mismatched marriage. This was why she wanted to give her marriage to Landon a chance.

"I just wanted to be sure we're on the same page, Jadin."

"We are," she confirmed. "We are both committed to this marriage. Look, I know you want a real marriage—one that includes sex, but I can't give you that just yet. I hope that you understand."

"I do."

Jadin smiled. "Can you say that with a little more conviction? Just a *little*?"

He laughed. "I understand, sweetheart."

They made small talk while they finished their tea.

Jadin stifled a yawn. "Oh, wow... I'm getting sleepy."

"That's a good thing," Landon responded. "Go on up. I'll see you in a few hours."

She stretched and yawned. "How much longer are you going to be down here?" There was a part of her that wasn't ready to leave his company, but it was getting late. She had to go into the office early because she was attending Millicent's funeral tomorrow afternoon.

"Not too long." He walked over to her, grabbed her hand and raised it to his lips. "Good night."

Jadin met his inscrutable gaze. His hand was still holding hers, his fingers warm and strong and protective.

Almost possessive.

Her legs suddenly felt unsteady, her breathing patchy, her heart skipping a beat as she felt the magnetic pull of his tall, strong presence drawing her inexorably closer. Jadin's acute awareness of Landon grew from deep inside her body, stirring all her dormant senses into wakefulness. Her inner core flickered with a pulse of sudden, insistent desire. It traveled through Jadin, making her aware of every part of her body, all the sensitive areas that longed for his touch.

Jadin wondered if Landon knew how much she wanted him. Could he read it in her face? In her eyes? In her body? Could he feel it in the electrically charged atmosphere?

"Do you want another cup of tea?" he asked.

His question cut into her thoughts. "Huh?"

"I asked if you wanted another cup of tea."

"Oh, no… I think I'll just grab some water. I need something cool to drink."

Jadin thought she caught a flash of amusement in his gaze.

Flushed, she opened the refrigerator and retrieved a bottled water. "See you in a few."

Millicent Witherspoon-Herndon was laid to rest on a rainy Wednesday afternoon. The church was filled with family, friends and spectators. News reporters camped outside, under huge umbrellas and tents. The cameras flashed a few rounds as soon as a journalist pushed a microphone toward Jadin as she left her car and walked up the steps of the church. "No comment," she said.

Jadin glanced around the sanctuary. She half expected Landon to be there, but he was not. The detectives investigating the case were present, however.

Jadin looked around for a seat, but the pews were filled. She locked eyes with a young woman with long ombré-colored hair in golden-honey shades of brown. The woman averted her gaze.

Jadin returned her attention toward the front, where roses, other colorful arrangements and plants surrounded Millicent's elaborate coffin.

Blaine sat stoically throughout the service. A couple of times, she caught sight of him dabbing his eyes with a handkerchief.

They left the church an hour later and traveled the short distance to the cemetery.

Jadin waited until Blaine was the only one standing at the grave.

He looked up as she approached. "Thank you for coming."

"Mr. Herndon, I'm so sorry for your loss."

"I can't believe Milli's gone," he whispered. "I keep thinking that one day I'm going to wake up and find out that this was just a horrible nightmare." He looked over his shoulder, then back at her. "I'm grateful I was able to get bail, or I wouldn't have been able to attend my wife's funeral."

He had been released after putting up two million dollars and surrendering his passport. "I am going to work hard to get this straightened out."

"I know you will," he responded with a tiny smile. "You represented my friend Vincent Tomlin."

"Yes, I did," Jadin said. She remembered the case. Vincent had been accused of embezzling money from his employer but was vindicated when the paper trail led to a disgruntled partner. He'd tried to cover his crime by trying to set up Vincent. "I thought I saw him earlier at the church."

"He was there."

"I have to get back to my office. I'll give you a call in a couple of days."

"Thank you, Jadin."


"How was the funeral?" Landon asked when she arrived home later that evening. "There were a lot of people there from the looks of it."

"It's been on all the local news channels. Millicent was loved by a lot of people," Jadin said. "Everyone had nothing but wonderful things to say about her. She touched so many lives."

"There was at least one person who hated her enough to take her life. The way Millicent was stabbed—it was done by someone filled with a lot of rage."

She agreed. Jadin just did not believe that that person was Blaine Herndon. She truly believed the man was innocent. She just had to prove it.

Jadin and Landon drove to her parent's home on Sullivan's Island for the DuGrandpre weekly Sunday dinner. They were in his SUV, and she could not help but appreciate the buttery softness of the leather as she melted down into the seat.

"When is Jordin's baby due?" he inquired.

"She's having twins. According to her doctor, they are due to arrive any moment."

"Wow."

"I'm so excited. I can't wait to meet them," Jadin gushed.

Landon turned off the highway at the sign for Sullivan's Island. "You've always loved children."

She smiled. "Wait until you meet my nephew, Emery. Landon, he's so adorable. And I have the cutest little cousins, Kai, Amya and R.J. Just to warn you, they come to the house and spend the night at least once a month."

"I'm looking forward to hanging out with them." When Jadin made no move to get out of the car, he asked, "You ready?"

"Better get it over with, huh?" she said, but Jadin looked far from convinced of that idea as she stepped out.

Landon took her hand in his as they stepped along the walkway.

"We're in this together."

Two little girls ran toward them with a little boy following close behind.

Jadin gave each of them hugs as she introduced Kai, Amya and Emery to Landon.

"This is Landon," she told them. "He's my hu—"

"He's your *boo*," Amya interjected with giggles.

Jadin glanced over at Landon, who threw back his head and laughed.

"Young lady, what are you talking about? What do you know about a *boo*? Landon is my husband."

"And her *boo*," he said. "I'm actually her *boo-thang*."

Kai and Amya cracked up with laughter.

"Auntie Jay," Emery said, "you have a husband? Where's he been?"

"I was in another state, working, but I live here now."

Emery looked up at him and asked, "What do I call you?"

"You can call me Uncle Landon or just Landon—it's up to you."

"I'ma call you Uncle Landon."

"They're here," her aunt bellowed from the porch. "Ryker, come meet Jadin's husband. Girls…Emery, it's time to go inside and wash up. C'mon now."

Jadin felt nervous laughter bubble up as the foyer quickly filled with her cousin Ryker's muscular frame and Austin. They both stood as tall as Landon. He kept his arm around her, and she grabbed onto his hand as

it wrapped around her waist, clinging to him as if he was an anchor.

Her anchor.

She didn't know what to say.

When her father walked into the foyer, Landon extended his hand to shake hands with Etienne. "Sir, I'm sorry for the way I handled this situation. I wasn't aware that I was taking everyone by surprise."

Her father smiled. "Welcome to the family, son."

Ryker seemed to relax slightly as they watched Etienne take Landon's hand and shake it, while Austin said, "I knew I'd see you again."

Jadin led him into the family room, where the rest of the family had gathered. Her mother was in the kitchen with Aubrie. "I'm going to see if Mom needs any help."

"Come sit beside me," Rochelle said to Landon. "I'd like to get to know my new nephew."

Jadin bit back a grin as she rushed into the kitchen. "Hey, y'all. What can I do to help?"

Eleanor looked up. "Hon, can you prepare the potato salad? Everything is over there in the bowl."

"Where's your hubby?" Aubrie asked as she mixed the macaroni and cheese.

"He's in there, talking to your mother."

She gasped. "And you just left him alone with her?"

"Shush now," Eleanor said. "You two behave. We're all curious about this man."

"Mom, this man's name is Landon. I know you're disappointed in me, but can we please find a way to get past this?"

"I just always thought we could talk about anything," Eleanor responded thickly.

"Mom, everything happened so fast and then it was over. I kept it to myself because it was too painful to talk about."

Eleanor surveyed Jadin's face. "It's clear that you loved him. Honey, I just don't understand why you gave up on your marriage so quickly."

"I couldn't handle him being in law enforcement. Back then, all I could think of was one day he wouldn't come home to me."

"That was the only reason you left?"

"I felt it was a big enough one," Jadin responded. "When Giselle lost her husband, it was like there were cops being killed everywhere. Then I heard about the two FBI agents who were shot down in Florida—it was just too much."

"I actually understand where she's coming from," Aubrie said. "It's why I don't date men in the military or in law enforcement. I'm not cut out to handle all that comes with it."

"Well, I think you made the right decision in giving your marriage this second chance, sweetie. I liked Michael as a person, but I never thought he was the right man for you."

Jadin eyed her mother. "Why do you say that?"

"It just seemed like you were always trying too hard to make the relationship work," Eleanor said as she arranged a stack of rolls on a serving platter. "Michael is a sweetheart, but he's set in his ways. He wouldn't bend, so you always had to compromise. For example, our family dinners—if he was in town, you'd be with him instead of your family."

"Michael wasn't a fan of being around a lot of

people. Even when he goes to his own family gatherings, he doesn't stay long."

"But that's not how you are," Aubrie interjected.

"No, I'm not," she admitted.

"Since we're being so honest," her mother said, "I have to confess that I'm relieved you're not marrying Michael. Once I got over the first shock, I thought that maybe this situation with Landon was God-ordained."

Jadin chuckled. "I don't know if I'd say all that."

"If you married Michael, you'd be moving to California, right? You would be away from all of your family. That would have disappointed your daddy."

She nodded. "Mom, I was going to propose opening up a DuGrandpre law office out there."

"But you would still be away from your family."

"Yes."

Eleanor checked on the last of the chicken in the fryer. "Landon knows how important family is to you, so he moved to Charleston without even saying a word to you beforehand."

"Michael works with his uncle."

"There is an Alexander-DePaul Hotel here in Charleston. They are all up and down the East Coast," Eleanor said. "I've met Malcolm and Barbara Alexander. They are as family-centered as we are. I'm sure something could've been worked out so that you could stay close to yours."

Her mother was right. The Alexander family was a close-knit one. They constantly tried to persuade Michael, but he had no interest. He was content seeing them during work hours and every now and then at family functions. His cousin Sage had once told her that Michael's father was the same way.

"Jadin, did you really want to move to Los Angeles?" Aubrie asked.

"I wanted to be with Michael, and if that was in LA...I was going."

Eleanor wiped her hands on a towel. "Dinner's ready. I guess you'd better go rescue Landon."

## Chapter 8

Landon sat next to Jadin at the dinner table, but he could not read her face as they all passed around bowls and platters, filling plates with her mom's fried chicken, macaroni and cheese, potato salad and green beans. It was comfort food at its finest, and he wouldn't mind coming to more Sunday dinners if the DuGrandpre women's cooking tasted as good as everything looked.

Etienne blessed the food.

Landon sampled the macaroni and cheese. "This is delicious. I've never had any that had a little kick to it."

"It's Aubrie's recipe," Jadin said. "She uses Colby, cheddar, Monterey Jack and cayenne pepper."

"Landon, do you golf?" Ryker asked. He was seated directly across from Jadin. "Austin and I are going on Saturday morning, if you'd like to join us."

"As a matter of fact, I do. Sure... I'd like to come."

He appreciated the effort her family was making in welcoming him into the family. His own family had not been as large, but they were also close. Losing his mother had been devastating, but Landon drew comfort in knowing that she had loved him dearly.

"Did you make some plates for Ethan and Jordin?" Etienne asked his wife. "I told them that I'd bring dinner."

Eleanor nodded. "It's already packed up and on the kitchen counter."

Rochelle cleared her throat softly before saying, "I've been trying to think of the best way to handle this little secret marriage situation—"

"Mom…" Aubrie interrupted. "This doesn't concern you."

"Yes, it does concern me and everybody in this room. Word is already getting around that Jadin's married to the deputy prosecutor. And if that's not enough, she's representing Blaine Herndon—the man her husband charged with murder. We need to just host a lavish reception. It will give people something else to talk about and settle any speculation about your marriage."

"Rochelle might be right," Eleanor said.

Jadin glanced over at Landon, who said, "I agree. I think people need to see us as a couple first, especially since we're on opposite sides of this case."

"This whole situation is going to keep us in the news all around," Jacques said as he removed the skin from his chicken. "High-profile case, husband and wife on opposing sides… It'll be good for business."

Rochelle looked at her husband. "Really? Is that all you think about?"

A cell phone rang.

"That's Jordin's ringtone. I'd better answer it." Jadin pushed away from the table and rushed to get the phone from her purse.

"Hey…"

Minutes later, she hung up and said, "They're at the hospital. Jordin's water broke."

"I'll stay here until the children finish eating," Garland said, "then take them home."

Ryker looked at his wife. "I can stay with the kids if you want to go to the hospital."

She smiled. "You go. I'll be fine."

Austin turned to his wife, who was five months pregnant. "What about you, Bree? You going to the hospital?"

"I'd like to be there for Jordin."

"I can take Emery home with me," Garland told them.

Landon took Jadin by the hand. "Do you want me to go with you?"

She nodded. "Yes. I'd like that."

Ten minutes later, they were on their way to Roper St. Francis Hospital.

"You okay?" Landon inquired.

Jadin nodded. "She sounded scared when I talked to her on the phone."

"I suppose that's normal. This is a new experience for Jordin. She's a first-time mother."

"Garland doesn't really like hospitals because of what happened when she had Kai. She met Ryker because of a mix-up. Their children were switched at birth."

Landon's eyebrows rose in surprise. "Really?"

"That's why their daughters are the same age and have the same birthday."

"I just assumed they were fraternal twins."

"Ryker isn't really fond of hospitals, either, but I know he's going because he intends to make sure it doesn't happen again. He's going to watch those babies like a hawk." Jadin gave a small laugh. "I'm sure the staff will be trying to figure out if he's the father."

Landon glanced at her. "I thought babies stay in the rooms with the mothers nowadays."

"They do. This hospital encourages rooming with the mother. They also have a lot of security measures in place."

The twenty-minute drive ended.

Landon and Jadin met up with the rest of her family in the hospital waiting area.

"I'll be out here if you need me," he told her. "Go be with your sister."

Jadin, Bree and her mother rushed to be at Jordin's side.

They found her with tears streaming down her face. "I have to have a C-section."

Ethan moved out of the way so that Eleanor could comfort her daughter.

"Oh, sweetie…"

"I told the d-doctor that I'd t-try to p-push harder," Jordin said between sobs.

"Honey, if they think a C-section is best, there's nothing wrong with delivering your babies this way." Eleanor wiped Jordin's face with a tissue. "You will still be able to bond with your babies and Ethan will be in there with you."

"How are you doing?" Jadin asked her brother-in-law.

"I'm fine. I'm just ready to see my babies." He looked down at her.

"It won't be long now," she assured him.

Lowering his voice, he asked, "Why is she so upset about having a C-section?"

Jadin gestured for him to step outside the room.

"Some mothers feel guilty over not being able to have their children naturally. I don't think I'd be one of those women, but I guess Jordin was really looking forward to the whole labor and screaming-her-head-off experience."

"I don't care how my babies are delivered," Ethan said. "I just want Jordin and them all healthy."

When it was time, Ethan went with Jordin to the delivery room.

Jadin, Bree and Eleanor made their way to the waiting area. She sat down beside Landon.

"How is Jordin?" he asked.

"She was upset because she has to have a C-section, but I think she was feeling better about it when they took her to the delivery room."

"The way that woman was screaming in the room next to Jordin's, I think I'd rather have the C-section," Bree said.

Austin kissed her cheek. "I got you, baby. We are going to breeze right through labor and delivery."

Eleanor smiled. "You keep up those pep talks, and Bree will do just fine."

Jadin looked at Landon. "What are you thinking about?"

"I'm imagining what it will be like when we have our first child. I think that you'll be very calm. You would've already made a list of everything months ahead of time. I'd be running through it in my mind, making sure I don't forget anything...like the car seat."

She laughed. "I believe you'll actually be the calm one. I have a very low tolerance for pain, so I won't be in a very good mood."

"That's where the foot massages and back rubs come in," Landon said.

"What do you know about that?"

"I've read books on pregnancy and parenting."

She was surprised. "Why?"

"Because one day, I will be a father. Like you, I don't like waiting till the last minute to try to figure out stuff."

"I suppose you've read books on marriage, too."

Landon nodded. "Unfortunately, none of them really applied to our unique situation."

She broke into a grin. "No, I guess they wouldn't."

An hour and a half later, she and Landon met their newborn niece and nephew.

"They are so adorable," Jadin murmured.

She looked up at her husband and Landon's eyes looked bright with tears.

"They're beautiful," he said.

"Do you want to hold them?" Jadin asked.

He shook his head no. "I'll wait until they get much bigger. Ethan Jr. looks like he'd fit in the palm of my hand."

"Erin... Hey, cutie," she whispered. "I'm so glad to see you."

They spent another hour at the hospital before going home.

"I should have packed up a couple of pieces of your mom's fried chicken," Landon said. "I'm hungry."

"I can make you a sandwich."

He kissed her. "I'll do it. You want one?"

"Sure."

Jadin followed him into the kitchen. She sat at the counter while Landon pulled packages of ham, cheese and condiments out of the fridge. "I remember the late-night grilled cheese sandwiches you used to make to get us through those study sessions. I don't think I've had one since I left law school."

Landon looked up at her. "Really?"

"It's true."

"I'll have to change that," he said while placing her sandwich in front of her.

When they finished eating, Jadin and Landon settled in the family room to watch television.

"I'm glad you were there with me at the hospital." Jadin knew that Michael never would have gone. He and Landon were so very different. It was a wonder that she could care for them both. She was realizing that her feelings for Michael did not run as deeply as she had thought.

Landon's laughter put an end to all thoughts of Michael.

Jadin turned her attention to the TV, as she drank in his nearness.

He placed an arm around her.

She felt wrapped in an invisible warmth. Jadin looked over at him, trying to assess his unreadable features.

Landon turned to face her. "What are you thinking about right now?" he asked.

"How much I've missed this... Us..." Jadin slowly brought her gaze up to his, her stomach dropping like a book toppling off the top shelf as his eyes meshed with hers. The feel of his fingers wrapping around her own was like a surge of electricity through her body, one she felt right to her core.

"We had a lot of good times."

She nodded in agreement.

"Jadin, we were meant for each other. I know right now you may have some reservations, but I intend to prove it to you."

She cleared her throat, pretending not to be affected by his words.

Landon gathered her in his arm and held her snugly. "I'm going to prove it to you, starting now."

His fingers loosened a fraction, but he did not release her. His eyes were dark and unreadable as they held hers. Before she realized what was happening, Landon kissed her.

He pressed gently against the lush fullness of her lips, relishing the softness of her mouth as it responded to his. Her lips were slightly parted, and he took full advantage of it.

Jadin gave herself freely to the passion of Landon's kiss.

Burying her face in his neck, she breathed a kiss there.

Landon recaptured her mouth, his tongue sending shivers of desire racing wildly through her.

His body responded to Jadin's closeness with a painful throb of primal need.

"Stop," she breathed raggedly, but his answer was to kiss her again. Jadin pulled away. "Landon, stop. Please."

He froze, struggling to breathe.

Finally, her eyes met his. They were wide, the pupils dark with arousal and tinged with fear. "I can't... It's just too soon."

"Can't?" He said it softly, but it came out strained.

She searched for the right words. "We have so much at stake, Landon. We are trying to rebuild our relationship and a marriage. I don't want to complicate it by rushing into sex."

He blinked slowly, holding her tethered with his eyes. "I take it that this means you want to make love, but you think it's too soon. Honey, it's not like we're dating. You're my wife."

"This is an awkward situation, I know."

"You're right, of course," Landon replied, his voice strangely thick. "We just got caught up in the moment."

"I think I'm just going to go take a bath—"

Landon cut her off by saying, "The image of you in a bathtub is definitely not what I need right now."

Jadin planted a quick kiss on his lips. "I'll see you in the morning." The fire that was ignited within her still burned. Part of her wanted to grab Landon by the hand and drag him upstairs. She wanted more of his slow, drugging kisses. She wanted *him*. Making love to him right now would only confuse matters more. Jadin had to keep a clear head if she wanted to make sure Landon was her happily-ever-after.

Uncontrollable.

Desire pulsed through Landon's body like a raging tide, pounding through his veins, swelling him, extending him until he was as trigger-happy as a teenager having sex for the first time.

Jadin's sweetness was intoxicating. If she hadn't

pulled away, Landon thought he would devour her right there on the sofa. He did not want to think of himself having so little control over his impulses. Especially since he remained celibate most of the past five years.

*She is my wife.*

Landon knew he had to be patient with Jadin. He could not expect her to just jump into bed with him so soon after breaking up with Michael. She was not that kind of woman and it was one of the qualities he loved about her.

He was also aware that she had to really sort out her feelings. Landon believed she loved him still, but that those feelings were buried deep down somewhere.

Landon showered, slipped on a pair of pajama pants and crawled into bed.

He could not get his mind off their kiss, could not stop reliving it. The way Jadin's lips had felt, the way his tongue had played with hers in such a tantalizing manner.

Landon smiled. If that kiss was any indication of whether their marriage had a real chance, then he had nothing to worry about.

After a long day at work, Jadin entered her home through the garage entrance. The first thing she noticed was the Crock-Pot on the counter. She lifted the lid and the appetizing smell of corned beef and cabbage wafted out. Her stomach rumbled in appreciation.

Landon strolled into the kitchen. "Hey, I didn't know you were home."

She kissed him. "I just got here."

"I hope you're hungry. I made your favorite… Well, it used to be your favorite."

"I still love corned beef and cabbage, Landon. Thank you, and yes—I'm starving. I'm gonna run up-stairs to change and I'll be right back."

They made small talk over dinner.

Jadin was touched by Landon's thoughtfulness and his willingness to share in the cooking and other household chores.

She had a lot of work to do, so while Landon was at the gym, she settled in her office.

Jadin had no idea how much time had passed. She hadn't heard Landon come back, so she assumed it couldn't be too late.

She stifled a yawn.

"Time for you to take a little break," Landon said, entering her office with a slice of pound cake and a steaming mug.

"Oh, goodness…" She accepted the hot drink. "Pep-permint tea?"

"Yes."

Jadin was touched and surprised that he had thought to get her something herbal. "Thanks. This was so thoughtful of you."

"My mom used to drink it all the time. She said that peppermint tea had a way of easing away any stress she was feeling."

"I've had a very stressful day. Mondays are always a challenge for me."

"I feel the same way," Landon said.

Jadin leaned back in her chair. "Blaine Herndon says that he didn't kill his wife and I believe him."

"Okay, let's just look at the facts," Landon re-sponded. "Around midnight, Millicent was stabbed ten times. Herndon was home but says that he never heard her scream. However, he does hear the house-keeper screaming the next morning."

"Doesn't make him a murderer." She bit into her cake. "This is sooo good."

"Jadin, why don't you ask to have the case reassigned?"

"Because I don't want to give it up. Landon, this is the type of case that can make or break my career."

"I can understand that," he said. "I just don't want this case to interfere with our marriage."

"Then don't let it."

"I won't if you agree to do the same."

Jadin nodded. She took a long sip of tea, then said, "Aunt Rochelle has decided to host a party for us."

"How does your mother feel about it?"

"Apparently, she's fine with the idea. She says it will give my aunt something other than the charity fund-raiser to focus on. Aunt Rochelle is driving my mom nuts. She and Mom can't agree on the theme."

Landon laughed. "I'd hate to get in between those two women."

"You and me both." Jadin finished off her cake.

"How much longer do you plan on working?"

She stretched and yawned. "I think I'm going to call it a night. What time is it anyway?"

"Almost one."

"Really?" Jadin opened her laptop to check the clock. "I didn't realize it was so late."

"Go on upstairs," Landon told her. "I'll be up shortly. Need to clean up the mess I made in the kitchen."

"Tell me something… Are you doing all this to impress me?"

He broke into a grin. "Is it working?"

# Chapter 9

The next day, Landon spent most of his morning going over every piece of evidence found at the Herndon house. He was surprised that there were not surveillance cameras installed inside the home, although he had been told that they were a fiercely private couple. The knife came from their kitchen. There was a lot of blood in the bedroom, but none on Herndon's clothing. Crime scene investigators were thorough but found no traces of any bloody clothes. A damp towel had been found on the floor of the master bathroom, confirming what Landon suspected—that Herndon must have been naked when he committed the heinous act. He'd then returned to the media room and slipped back into his clothes.

From all accounts, Herndon loved his wife. Everyone agreed that Millicent had appeared to be very happy in her marriage. They had even planned to take a trip to Greece later this year as a second honeymoon. Herndon bought the tickets a month ago.

Landon frowned. Why would he buy airline tickets if he had planned to kill her? Unless, he purchased them just to throw the investigation off track.

He left the office at six o'clock. Landon was looking forward to seeing Jadin.

Music was playing softly when he entered the house, and the table was set for two, but Jadin was nowhere to be found.

He smiled. Now she was trying to impress him.

He walked upstairs and there Jadin was, dripping with moisture and half-naked.

"I—I didn't expect you to be home so early." She carefully wrapped the white towel tighter around her. "I was making dinner. When I got out of the shower, the timer was going off. I have chicken in the oven."

He sat his attaché case on the floor, outside his bedroom. "I'll take care of it."

"Thank you," she murmured before rushing off to her room.

When she came downstairs, Jadin was dressed in a pair of jeans and a tank top. Her damp hair was pulled up in a ponytail.

"I see you've learned to cook."

"Ha. Ha," she responded. "I picked up a few things from my mom and my cousin."

"I like Aubrie's restaurant," he said. "I'm addicted to the bread pudding."

Jadin smiled. "I know. Everybody loves it."

Right before they sat down to eat, her cell phone began vibrating.

Jadin picked it up. "I'm sorry. I really need to take this call."

She disappeared up the stairs.

When she returned, Jadin had changed into a pant-suit and had her hair pinned neatly into a bun. "Something's come up and I need to meet with a client. Sorry about abandoning you like this."

"It comes with the job. I understand."

She blew a kiss in his direction. "I'll be back as soon as I can."

Jadin had agreed to meet Blaine Herndon at the law firm. She called ahead to notify the building security that he would be coming. She also knew that there would be DuGrandpre attorneys and paralegals working late hours, especially if they were preparing for trials.

He was in the lobby, waiting, when she arrived. Blaine Herndon might be a billionaire, but he had none of the trappings of old money. He was a self-made man. He was not wearing some custom-designed suit, choosing instead a pair of well-worn jeans and a crisp linen shirt.

"Hello, Mr. Herndon."

"Thank you for seeing me."

"It sounded more like an order than a request," Jadin said flatly as she walked with him to the elevator.

"I apologize. I sometimes forget that I don't have to bark orders at everyone."

"Why did you insist on seeing me at this late hour?" Jadin asked when they entered a conference room.

The office was oddly silent. No ringing phones. No one putting their head around the door with questions or requests. The only sound for what seemed like minutes—but was only seconds—was the pounding beat of her pulse in her ears.

Finally, Blaine decided to cut into the silence. "There's something you need to know. Millicent and I had a good marriage, and I loved her..." he began. "A year ago, I met a flight attendant named Sandra. She and I..."

"You were having an affair."

Blaine nodded. "I never intended on leaving Millicent. In fact, I ended my relationship with Sandra a couple of months ago."

Jadin began to relax as she made notes while they talked. "Did you have a prenup?"

"Yes. Millicent would get a five-hundred-million-dollar settlement if the marriage ended." He paused for a moment before continuing. "Jadin, I'm telling you the truth. I did not kill my wife. Someone came into our home that night. I haven't told the detectives about Sandra because I knew how it would look to them. Milli and I were going on a second honeymoon in the fall. We were going to Greece." His eyes filled with unshed tears.

"Investigators are going to find out about Sandra eventually. You know that?"

He nodded. "That's why I wanted to tell you first. I was very discreet, but... I'm hoping this doesn't have to come out. Because if it does, I'm sure you have an idea of what will happen. It's already a freaking media show out there. Everybody's tweeting about me and trying to determine if I'm guilty or not."

"Take me back over that night, Mr. Herndon."

"Call me Blaine."

Jadin gave a slight nod. "What happened, Blaine?"

"We had gone out to dinner… I guess it was around seven o'clock. We came home and sat down in the media room to watch a movie. Milli opened a bottle of Pierre Pierot Cristal Brut. After a couple of glasses, Milli started to feel bad… One of her migraines. She went upstairs… I fell asleep. Next thing I hear is Rosa screaming and feeling like I was in a fog."

She stopped writing. "Your wife was fine during dinner?"

He nodded. "Milli really enjoyed her meal. We had a great time."

"Blaine, I have to ask this question… Do you know if your wife was happy? Could she have found out about your affair?"

"If Milli knew anything about Sandra, she would've said something. She wasn't the type of woman to keep quiet and suffer in silence. I would've been served with divorce papers already."

"Is it possible that she was seeing someone?"

"I guess it's possible, but I'm pretty sure that she wasn't. Like I said, Milli wasn't the type of woman to sit still on something like that. If she wasn't happy with me, she would have left."

"What would she have gotten if she filed for divorce with no real justification, such as abuse or adultery?" Jadin asked.

"Five million dollars, the house in Hilton Head and the vacation home in Maui."

Jadin knew that Blaine was worth billions. He was one of the top ten richest men in the country. "Millicent's murder could not be about the money," she reasoned. The amount involved, though admittedly large, was peanuts to a man of his wealth.

"Where does Sandra live?"

"She lives in Savannah. I haven't seen her in a couple of months. It's over between us."

"Has she ever been in your house?"

"Only once," Blaine responded. "Milli was in Hawaii with her friends. The minute I brought her here, I knew it was wrong, so we left. I took her to a hotel."

*A cheating husband with morals.*

As if he could read her thoughts, Blaine said, "I know what you must think."

"It doesn't matter what I think," Jadin stated. "I'm here to represent you and I'm going to do just that."

"How long have you and Landon Trent been married?"

"Five years."

"I had no idea that you had a husband." He pointed at her left hand. "You don't wear a wedding ring."

"We were separated."

"So, you've decided to work things out, then?"

"Yes, we have." Jadin looked down at her notes. "Are you normally such a heavy sleeper?"

"That's what is so strange about that night. Usually, I wake up at the slightest sound. When I travel, I use earplugs or I'll be waking up all through the night."

"Even when you drink?"

Blaine scratched his cheek. "It depends on how much I've had. Milli and I had several glasses of champagne that night. We'd had some at the restaurant, then opened the bottle that Milli said came earlier in the day from one of my business associates. Milli loves champagne, but when she drinks too much, she will sometimes develop a headache."

"Who sent you the champagne?"

"I'm not really sure," Blaine responded. "Milli opened the box when it arrived."

When Jadin had first met with Blaine, she was not entirely sure she believed in his innocence, but it did not matter. She was hired to defend him and even if he were truly guilty, she would do her job. But now, she had to admit that she had some reservations regarding his guilt.

He had been unfaithful, but Jadin believed that he loved his wife.

"How did your meeting go?" Landon asked when she returned home.

"It was pretty good," she responded. "I didn't expect to be gone as long as I was, though."

He kept her company while she ate.

"Do you often have meetings this late?"

"Not really," Jadin said. "But this is one I had to take."

"Blaine Herndon," Landon responded. "You met with him."

"He's my client." Jadin thought she detected a bit of jealousy in his tone. She bit back a smile.

"He may be guilty of murder."

"Landon, he may also be innocent," she pointed out. "We met at the firm. I had security and coworkers surrounding me. I wasn't in any danger." She finished off her iced water. "I appreciate you worrying about me, though."

"I care about you, Jadin. That has never changed. Not for me anyway."

She reached over and covered his hand with her own. "Landon, I care about you, too."

His eyes roved over her seductively. "I'm so tired of taking cold showers."

"If it makes you feel any better, I'm really enjoying our time together. I actually look forward to coming home to you…"

Landon smiled. "That makes me feel a whole lot better." He kissed her. "Thanks, sweetheart."

When he walked into the family room, she studied his lean, muscled body and whispered under her breath, "Lord, I can't keep this up much longer."

Landon stood behind the center island, waiting for his coffee to brew. He was still wearing his running shorts and T-shirt from his morning run.

He smiled at the unexpected sight of her. "Morning, Jadin. What are you doing up so early?"

"I need to take care of some things at the office." She took an orange from the refrigerator and started to peel it, holding the garbage can open with one foot as she tossed the peels. When she was finished, she climbed onto one of the bar stools at the kitchen island.

"Can you meet me at my office around eleven?" Landon asked. "I want to discuss the Herndon case."

"Are you thinking about putting a deal on the table?"

"My boss wants me to—he doesn't want this case tried in the public and played out in the news."

"I'll be there."

She stepped down and said, "I need to get ready to get out of here."

The scent of her was beyond description. Somewhere between heaven and bliss, Landon tried his best to inhale her when she walked past him. He watched Jadin leave the kitchen and realized he could not live with this woman for a year and not be able to make love to her.

He left for work minutes after Jadin.

Landon intended to offer Herndon a sentence plea deal—it would guarantee him a conviction and Herndon would have the death penalty taken off the table. However, he would have to serve a minimum of thirty-five years in prison with no parole or reduction in time served. It was the best Landon could offer, considering the first-degree murder charge.

He spent part of his morning with his boss, who wanted the Herndon case to go away. Millicent Witherspoon-Herndon's murder was a heavy weight hanging over Charleston.

"Knock…knock…" Jadin said from the hallway. "Can I come in?"

Nodding, he gestured for her to enter.

"Landon, Blaine didn't kill his wife," she said as she sank down in the chair facing his desk.

"How can you be so sure?"

"Because they were going on a second honeymoon. This man loved Millicent. I could see it in his eyes."

"I know about the tickets and he could've purchased them to cast suspicion off him."

Disagreeing, Jadin shook her head. "I'm not going to advise my client to plead guilty to something he didn't do, Landon. You don't have any evidence to support this murder charge. He is a self-made billionaire who generously gave his wife whatever she desired. This crime wasn't about money. I'm sure you have her bank records. He gave her a very nice allowance each month."

"You are aware that he had a prenup."

"She would have gotten millions," Jadin said. "And two homes."

Landon shook his head. "None of this is making any sense."

"I agree."

He looked at her. "The only deal I can offer is thirty-five years minimum. If he goes to trial, Herndon could end up with a life sentence."

"You know I'm not going to agree to this. I will mention it to my client, but I'm positive we will take our chances with the jury." She picked up her tote. "I'll see you at home."

"Don't hold dinner for me. I'll probably be here pretty late tonight."

"Oh, okay, then."

Jadin felt a prick of disappointment that he wouldn't be home when she got there. She looked forward to sharing meals with him.

She ran into her brother outside the building that housed the DuGrandpre law offices.

"Where are you coming from?" Austin inquired.

"Landon offered a plea deal. If Blaine confesses to murdering his wife, the death penalty and life sentence are off the table. He'll get the minimum."

"Thirty-five years?"

Jadin nodded. "If I believed he was guilty, I'd advise him to take it, but I don't think he did it. He loved his wife."

"I heard you met with him last night."

"We went over that night again."

"Has his story changed?"

"Not at all. They went to dinner, drank champagne…

went home and drank more. His wife had a headache and went to bed. He fell asleep in the media room. Woke up to the housekeeper screaming. One thing he said to me was that when he travels, he takes earplugs with him because he's a light sleeper."

"That's doesn't mesh with him not hearing anything that night."

They took the elevator to the fourth floor.

"It almost sounds like he was drugged or something," Jadin murmured.

"Did the investigators go over everything?" Austin asked. "They were drinking, so maybe he was drunk. Who would have drugged him?"

"The bottle of champagne came from one of his business associates—that's what Millicent told him. It had been delivered earlier in the day." She looked at Austin. "That bottle should be tested."

He followed her into her office. "So, you really think that they were drugged?"

"Think about it, Austin. Blaine never heard his wife scream. What if she didn't? Maybe she was too drugged to even know what was happening to her." Jadin picked up her phone. "I need that bottle. We can have our investigators test it."

"That's if the police didn't take it."

"Blaine, this is Jadin. Can you tell me what happened to the bottle of champagne from that night?"

"I think the police have it. Why?"

"Do you know of anyone who would want to see your wife dead?"

"No. Everyone loved Milli." He paused for a moment, then asked, "Jadin, what's going on?"

"I think you may have been drugged," she responded.

"A drug like Rohypnol is tasteless, odorless and can knock you out. The other thing is that it can also cause amnesia. This is the only thing that makes sense to me, especially if you're normally a light sleeper."

"I can go to my doctor and get tested if that will help."

"Yes, please do that," Jadin said. "But it will be a long shot since this drug doesn't stay in your system for longer than seventy-two hours."

"Is that why you want the bottle of champagne?"

"Hopefully, once they test it, that will confirm my suspicions. However, we are still without a suspect. Unless you kept the packaging it came in."

"I don't think so. Milli probably threw it away."

"Will you look anyway?" Jadin said.

She called Detective Solomon next. "Mike, hey... It's Jadin." She and Mike had grown up together on Sullivan's Island. His parents were close friends of Etienne and Eleanor.

"Hello. What can I do for you?"

"I need to know if the champagne bottle that was in the Herndon's media room has been tested for prints or anything else."

"Why?"

"Mike, that bottle was a gift. It was delivered earlier in the day to the house. Millicent told Blaine that it was from one of his business associates."

"Are you trying to tell me that you think the person who sent the champagne should be considered a suspect?" He laughed. "You're kidding me, right?"

"Mike, I think Blaine and his wife were drugged. Have the bottle tested."

"Jadin, I think you're reaching on this one."

"Mike..."

"Okay. I'll check it out."

She hung up. "I guess we'll see if any of this pans out."

"Jadin, trust your instincts," Austin recommended.

"I'm glad you're working this case with me. This is the biggest case of my career. I don't want to make any stupid mistakes."

"This is the biggest case of Landon's career, as well."

"I know," Jadin said. "If I can prove Blaine is innocent and point him in the direction of the real murderer, we both win."

Shaking his head, Austin chuckled. "Looks like Landon is gonna stay my brother-in-law."

She grinned. "If everything stays the way it is now, I agree."

"Hey, Mama…"

Jordin broke into a grin. "I'm so glad to see you. I'm starving for some adult conversation."

"They are just so adorable," Jadin murmured as she gazed at her niece and nephew. "Oh, my goodness. I could stay here and love on them all day." She looked back at her sister. "You are so lucky, Jordin."

"I love my babies so much, but I'm not used to being home all day like this. But I don't want to leave them, either."

"Your hormones are all over the place."

Jordin agreed. "I think I'm driving Ethan nuts. One minute I'm fine, then the next thing I'm crying." She glanced up at her sister. "So, how's married life?"

"I don't know. I feel like Landon and I are just roommates. We get along great. We always have."

"So, you don't feel anything for him...like sexual?"

"I didn't say that, Jordin."

"Then what's the problem?"

"He's sleeping in the guest room."

"I know Landon didn't want that," Jordin said. "That's all you."

"I suppose you think I should have just let him into my bed from the moment he moved in."

"He *is* your husband, Jadin. You don't feel married because you two aren't acting like a married couple. I hope it's not because of Michael, because he should be a nonfactor at this point."

Jadin gently stroked Erin's silky hair. "You are such a sweetie," she whispered.

"Are you listening to me?" Jordin asked.

"I heard you." Jadin looked up at her sister. "I'm still very much attracted to Landon. I look forward to seeing him when I get home. We have so much fun... It just feels right. But then I think about Michael."

*"And?"*

"And I realize just how different he and I were," Jadin responded. "Landon and I are more kindred spirits. I'd forgotten what that feels like."

"Then why don't you give your marriage a real chance?"

"You're right. I really haven't been fair to Landon. He's been so wonderful and patient."

Jordin grinned. "So do yourself a favor and give the man a treat."

Her sister's words stayed at the forefront of her mind for the rest of the day.

That evening, when she walked in and saw Landon in his gym clothes, it was a lot more than Jadin could handle. His T-shirt looked soft and comfortable, as if it had been washed hundreds of times. It was well-worn and threadbare with see-through spots that gave a hint of the skin underneath. It was still slightly damp from his workout, so it clung to his abs, showing off the cut of each muscle on his stomach.

It would be impossible to say whether it was the shudder that ran through Jadin, her tongue moistening her full lower lip or the tiny moan low in her throat that precipitated what happened next.

As Landon's lips touched hers, it was like oxygen to the fire that had been smoldering for weeks.

"I've... I've been thinking that it's time for you to move into the master bedroom."

"Are you sure about this?" he asked, staring into her eyes.

"Yes," she whispered. "If we want a real marriage..."

"That's what I want." The words came out in a rush.

Before she realized what was happening, Landon had picked her up and was carrying her through the house and up the stairs.

In the room, he laid her on the bed.

Landon sat down on the edge. "I need to know if this is what you really want, Jadin."

Jadin sat up against a set of pillows. "We said we were going to try to make this work. We can't do that in separate bedrooms. I see that now."

"I'm glad because I was feeling more like your roomie than your husband," Landon said.

She gave him a playful pinch. "Why didn't you say something?"

"Jadin, I didn't want you to feel pressured."

"I've been so unfair to you, Landon. You have been so sweet and loving... I'm not sure I deserve you."

"I love you, Jadin. I've never stopped."

"Come here," she told him.

He climbed all the way into the bed.

Landon's arms encircled her, one hand on the small of her back.

Jadin settled back, enjoying the feel of his arms around her. "I can't begin to tell you how much I've missed you."

"Don't tell me... Show me..."

Passions spent, Landon and Jadin lay in bed, legs entwined.

"Why didn't you come after me sooner?" she asked.

"Because I knew I'd have to choose between the job I loved and you," Landon replied in earnest. "Sweetheart, I wasn't ready to do that."

Jadin looked up at him. "That almost makes me feel as if I wasn't enough for you."

"It wasn't that at all. I knew you would never be happy away from your family. Eventually, you would've resented me, and I couldn't live with that. I knew that I would have to come to Charleston if I wanted a real chance with you."

"I used to think that you were too good to be true, Landon. I would tell myself that no man is this perfect. I was convinced when I left you—no man ever came close to the man that you are."

Landon wanted to ask about her relationship with Michael but decided now was definitely not the right time for that. He did not want to bring him back into their lives—or the memory of him in her bed.

Jadin laid her head on his chest. "I hope the rest of our lives feel like it does in this very moment."

"How is that?"

"It's hard to explain. This just feels like home. Home is a refuge, a safe and loving place… It's fun, happy…"

He kissed her. "Home to me is love, security and a connection."

"Exactly, it isn't as much a place as a feeling," Jadin said. "When I'm with you, I feel like I'm home."

Landon gazed into her eyes. "I feel the same way, sweetheart." His heart turned in response to the tender smile on her face.

They had only been back together for a few weeks. Had she completely erased Michael from her heart? Landon wanted to believe that Jadin realized her feelings for the man were not what she thought they were, yet he could not forget that she had accepted Michael's proposal. Her feelings ran deeply enough for her to consider marriage.

Landon refused to let doubt creep into his thoughts. He had never known Jadin to be flighty, so he had to trust that she knew who and what she wanted.

# Chapter 10

"Why didn't you tell me about your theory?" Landon asked when Jadin arrived home.

"You talked to Mike?"

"You think Herndon was set up? Sweetheart, you can't be serious about this. It just makes sense that he murdered his wife."

"I'm very serious," Jadin responded. "Landon, you have no real evidence to support *your* theory other than the fact that Blaine was home when his wife was stabbed to death."

"Okay, let's say you're right about the champagne. How do you know Herndon didn't roofie his own wife?"

"He also drank from the same bottle. I'm sure if you test the champagne glasses, you'll find the drug or whatever there, as well. Landon, there is so much more to this story than you, I or even Blaine knows. I'm sure of it." Jadin already had urine samples taken from Blaine sent to an independent lab the firm had used in the past. She wanted to verify there were no traces of any drugs in his system.

He did not seem convinced.

"I guess we'll both know I'm right when Mike gets the results back," Jadin stated. "I'm gonna change clothes, then I have some work to do."

He gave her a quick kiss, then picked up his keys. "I put your food in the microwave. I'll be leaving in a few to go to the gym. Don't work too late."

Jadin stared with longing at Landon. "I'll get what I can done while you're working out. When you get back...all my attention belongs to you."

He looked her over seductively. "I'll be back in an hour."

"You were right," Landon said when Jadin picked up the phone the next day. "Traces of Rohypnol were found in the glasses and in the champagne bottle."

She leaned back in her chair. "I knew it. *I knew it.*"

"This isn't enough evidence to let Blaine off the hook for this murder."

"It's a start," she responded.

"You really believe in his innocence, don't you?"

"I do."

"Why?"

"He loved Millicent. I could hear it in his voice. I could see it in his eyes. His grief is pure and sincere."

"I have to go, but I'll see you later."

"Okay. Thanks for letting me know."

When he ended the call, Landon picked up the Herndon file, rose to his feet and strode into his boss's office.

"Herndon and his wife were drugged."

"What?"

"Lab results came back positive for Rohypnol." He sat down in a nearby chair. "When I observed Herndon's initial interview, I thought he seemed a bit off. Now it makes sense."

"Do you think he's innocent?"

"I can't say that," Landon responded. "This could be an elaborate ruse on his part to cover up his tracks. I understand that this bottle of champagne was a gift. If so, it was from someone who knew that this brand was a favorite of the Herndons."

"How did they get into the house?"

"He could've let them in. He was downstairs." Landon paused, then said, "A side effect of Rohypnol is amnesia. That's why it's a favorite date-rape drug. Most victims don't remember what happened. He could've had a visitor and not remembered."

"You need to find out who sent the champagne."

Landon rose to his feet. "I'm on it. I'll give Mike a call now."

The DuGrandpre party held in Jadin and Landon's honor arrived the second Saturday in June. Rochelle had done a splendid job with the decor.

Landon looked so handsome in his tuxedo. Jadin could hardly take her eyes off him.

"I know maybe five or six of our guests outside of your family," he whispered in her ear. "Do you know all these people?"

She laughed. "No, I don't. Aunt Rochelle says it's not

a party if there aren't at least a hundred people in attendance."

"Aubrie outdid herself with the food."

Jadin agreed. Everything had turned out perfectly. Even Jordin and Ethan came but did not stay long. The twins were four weeks old, so they did not want to be away for too long, although they were in the care of Ethan's mother.

"This evening was perfect," she said. "This is what we missed when we eloped.

Family, friends…"

"We can always do it again," Landon suggested. He fingered the thin strap of the purple gown she was wearing. "You look so beautiful. I love this color on you."

"Thank you for the compliment," she said. "Yeah, I guess we could renew our vows one day. I think it would really make my mother happy. Maybe she'd finally forgive me for eloping."

Landon pulled her off to the side. "I have something for you."

"What is it?"

He pulled out a black velvet box. "I know that we said we didn't need rings, but every time I look at your hand, it makes me realize just how much I want to see my ring on your finger."

Jadin looked at the cushion-cut diamond wedding set. "Landon, it's beautiful."

He tenderly placed it on her left ring finger.

She broke into a grin. "You know your left hand looks a little bare. I know you're mine, but like you, I want to see that same symbol of love on your finger."

She pulled a tiny box out of her clutch. "We are still very much in sync, Landon."

He laughed.

Jadin placed his wedding band on his finger.

Applause interrupted this special moment between them.

"It's about time y'all put a ring on it," Ryker said.

Jadin and Landon burst into another round of laughter.

She had to admit that their wedding rings signified a deeper connection. She and Landon were becoming closer. Jadin knew without a doubt that he was her Mr. Right. He was her soul mate.

# Chapter 11

Landon touched his mouth to hers. "Jadin." He murmured it, giving her hand a tug until she rested more closely against his chin.

She shuddered as he leaned down, covering her mouth with his. Jadin moved her head, silently asking for more.

She turned her head toward his and he brushed light kisses against her jaw. When her weight shifted slightly, he let his hand slide to cradle her ribs intimately.

With his right arm, Landon pressed gently, until she turned into his body. His breath came out with a rush and he pulled her up, so she lay firmly atop him, his hand threading through her hair to hold her head in place while his tongue swept into her mouth.

Jadin felt her world suddenly spin out of control. Landon's kiss was filled with burning passion, and she felt a tingling sensation run through her body. Heat spread through her whole body.

"I don't want this night to ever end," Landon whispered.

"There will be many more nights like this," she assured him. "We have forever."

"Jadin, I didn't expect to see you," Blaine said when he answered the door.

She entered the foyer. "There's something…" Her voice died at the sight of the woman approaching them. Jadin initially thought she might be a relative, but the look the stranger had given her—she was pretty sure this woman did not share his DNA.

He looked at Jadin and said, "This is Sandra Davis. She was in town, heard about Millicent and came by to offer her condolences."

She was at the funeral, Jadin thought silently.

"This is my attorney, Jadin DuGrandpre."

Sandra blinked and then smiled but it did not reach her eyes. She extended her hand. "It's a pleasure to meet you."

Jadin was not fooled at all by the gesture. Nevertheless, she shook Sandra's hand. "Blaine, I have to get back to my office for a meeting. Can you come by around three o'clock? There's something I need to discuss with you."

"Sure, but we can talk now."

She glanced over at Sandra. "It's fine. I'll see you at three."

"I found the packaging the champagne came in," Blaine said. "I'll bring it with me."

"I can take it now," Jadin responded. "I can drop it off to the lab on the way back."

Sandra suddenly appeared nervous. She shifted from one foot to the other. "What is she talking about?"

"Someone sent me a bottle of champagne the day my wife died." He walked away, leaving the two women alone.

Jadin surveyed Sandra's face. She thought she detected a flash of fear in her gaze.

"Why do you need that? What's that got to do with his case?"

"It could be nothing, but I have to exhaust all avenues."

Before Sandra could respond, Blaine returned. "Here you go."

Reaching for the doorknob, Jadin said, "I'll leave you with your guest."

Sandra's reaction became her focus as she drove back to her office. The woman looked as if she was trying to maintain her composure, but something had spooked Sandra.

Jadin found herself checking the clock often. She had believed Blaine when he told her that he ended his affair. Now she was not sure what to think. His wife had only been gone a little over a month, and now he had Sandra in her home.

*There may be more to the story than what I saw*, Jadin reminded herself. She knew better than to make snap judgments.

As soon as the receptionist notified her of Blaine's arrival, she went out to get him.

The minute they were behind closed doors, Blaine said, "I know what you must be thinking, but I swear to you that I didn't know Sandra was even in town, much less that she would come by my house, Jadin. I hadn't seen her since we broke up."

She stared him straight in the face. "Blaine, you don't have to lie to me."

"Lie…about what? What are you talking about?"

"I saw her at Millicent's funeral."

"You must be mistaken," he responded. "Sandra was working a flight to Los Angeles."

"Is that what she told you?"

"Yes. We were talking about the dream I had of her."

"Dream?" Jadin had no idea what Blaine could possibly be talking about.

"I dreamed she came to the house and we had a terrible argument because Milli was upstairs. I kept telling her to leave… When I mentioned it to Sandra, she just laughed and said that there was no way it could have taken place because she was working the LA route at the time everything happened." He shook his head. "It seemed real, but I know it can't be."

Jadin met his gaze. "How did she take it when you ended the relationship?"

"She wasn't happy about it," he said. "Sandra wanted me to leave Milli. I told her that would never happen. Why do you ask?"

"You're a widower now."

"I would never marry Sandra. I enjoyed her company, but I was never in love with her."

"Did you tell her that?"

"No," Blaine responded. "I care about Sandra. But I don't want to hurt her."

*She might want to hurt you.* Jadin left the thought

unspoken. "The lab results came back, and traces of Rohypnol were found in the champagne you were sent."

"The date-rape drug?"

Jadin nodded. "I called Jordan and Associates—Kevin Jordan denies ever sending anything to your home."

"If he laced it with a drug, Kevin wouldn't just come out and say he sent it."

"We're having it scanned for fingerprints. Is Pierre Pierot Cristal Brut the only brand you drink?"

"Pretty much."

"Would Kevin know this?" Jadin inquired.

"Not really. He and I only see each other at business functions—not socially. I can't see him sending me such an expensive gift, now that I think about it. In fact, he's not especially fond of me."

"I got the same impression when I spoke with him," she said with a tiny smile.

"Milli and I had planned to attend the charity fundraiser hosted by your family on Saturday," Blaine said at the end of their meeting. "I don't think I should come with everything that's happened, but I still want to donate."

He pulled an envelope out of his pocket. "Please give this to your mother."

Jadin took the sealed envelope from Blaine. "Thank you."

When he left, she went to Austin's office.

"I need to run a scenario by you." Jadin sank down in one of the visitor chairs.

"What is it?"

"Let's say that Blaine was involved with someone... another woman. He ended the relationship because he never had any intentions of leaving his wife. The other woman is so upset that she comes up with a way to get rid of her competition."

"Was he involved with someone else?"

Jadin nodded. "A woman named Sandra Davis. He ended it a couple of months before the murder." Since Austin was working this case with her, she was free to discuss any pertinent information with him.

Arms folded, Austin asked, "Why do you think she's got something to do with this?"

"She lied to Blaine. I saw her at Millicent's funeral, but he believes she was working. Sandra told him that she was working the Savannah to Los Angeles route at that time."

"We can easily check that out."

"I know," Jadin said. "The other thing is that I called the person who supposedly sent Blaine and Millicent the bottle of Pierre Pierot Cristal Brut. It was clear this man couldn't stand Blaine. He said he wouldn't send Blaine a bottle of water, much less an expensive bottle of champagne. Besides, he and Blaine don't run in the same social circles—how would he know that this is a favorite brand of the Herndons? It's not like they're friends. But you know who *would* know? His girlfriend. I'd bet he stocked bottles of it at her home."

"She does have everything to gain," Austin said. "The woman who was standing between them is now dead. He is free to marry her."

"Exactly," Jadin responded. "The other thing is this... Blaine said they were talking about a dream he had—in it she came to the house and they argued because his wife was upstairs. I'm beginning to think that dream is more of a memory from that night."

"Do you really think this woman is capable of murder?"

"When I went to see him earlier at the house—she was there."

"Really?"

Jadin nodded. "When I asked for the packaging the champagne came in, Sandra acted a bit strange. She wanted to know why I wanted it and what it had to do with the case. She looked a little scared."

"Interesting."

"Very," Jadin responded. "We need to learn more about Sandra Davis."

The open buffet near the pool was spectacular. The laughter of the patrons and the sound of reggae music playing softly in the background was enticing. The sound of the ocean nearby was inviting. But it was the delicious aroma of jerk chicken, curried goat and other delicious entrées that really got Jadin's senses going. Her mother and aunt had done a wonderful job coordinating this charity event.

"Thank you," Jadin said as Landon pulled out a chair for her at the table with her parents.

"No problem, mon," he responded in a fake Jamaican accent.

She grinned and shook her head. "You're still corny."

Jadin couldn't remember the last time she had felt this way or had so much fun. Her senses were heightened in his presence. Like the pool and the sea, Landon was like a breath of fresh air. There was just something about him that connected with her magnetically. It was almost surreal.

A waiter brought tall drinks to the table that Landon had ordered a minute ago.

Pineapple cola with a slice of lemon, topped off with an umbrella.

When they went to the buffet table, Jadin got a spoonful of rice, a dab of curried goat and some ox-tail on the side with rice and peas to sample.

While she ate, Jadin swayed to Bob Marley's "One Love" blaring through the speakers.

"This is such a relaxing view, don't you think?"

"There's something calming about being near a body of water," Landon said in a low, deep voice.

"It's beautiful isn't it?" Jadin said, mesmerized by the serenity of the ocean view.

"I could stare at it all day," they both said in unison.

She looked at Landon and laughed.

Jadin finished drinking her pineapple cola as she rocked to the music, looking deeply into Landon's sexy eyes.

"Looks like you're ready to dance."

"I am."

"Go," her mother encouraged. "You two have fun."

Later that evening, they took a walk on the beach and listened to the powerful waves of the sea. The sky was a beautiful shade of purple and rouge.

Jadin snuggled into Landon's shoulder as they walked on the beach until the red sky turned to an awesome midnight blue sky, with the moon reflecting on the water and the backdrop of stars sprinkled against the sky.

A perfect night for lovers.

# Chapter 12

Jadin sank down in a tub of bubbly water, scented with lavender bath salts. It had been a long day and she was exhausted. She trailed her fingers in the hot liquid, playing with the bubbles. Picking up the bar of soap that sat in a dish beside the tub, she bathed.

"That looks inviting." His gaze roved to the creamy expanse of her neck and traveled downward.

She looked up at Landon. "Unfortunately, this tub was not made for two."

"We'll have to do something about that," he responded with a seductive grin.

"Can you check on the salmon? It should be done by now."

"You're trying to get rid of me."

"I'm sure you don't want our dinner to burn, because if it does, then you're taking me out to a restaurant of my choosing. I'm not settling for pizza like before."

Landon chuckled. "I'll go check on the salmon."

"Thanks, baby."

A few minutes later, Jadin got out and dried off with a soft, fluffy towel. She picked up a bottle of scented body lotion and slathered it on her skin.

She slipped on a sundress and went downstairs.

The first thing that caught her eyes were the dozen roses on the counter. "You bought me flowers?"

"Of course, I did."

He was the only man who had ever bought her flowers. Michael considered them a waste of money. Jadin decided from this moment forward that Michael was a part of her past. He did not deserve even a small part of her heart. He was a good man—just not the man for her. Her future was with Landon.

She walked up to him. "I love you."

He seemed caught off guard by her words. "I was wondering if I'd ever hear you say those words to me again. You've shown me that you love me, but I wanted to hear you say it."

"I love you, baby."

Landon kissed her. "I love you, too. More than you could possibly know."

After dinner by candlelight, they sat on the porch.

The moonlit view was spectacular but so was the view of Landon's physique every time she stole glances at him. It was nice to be with someone who respected her choices and loved her for who she was. Someone who did not ridicule her romantic gestures. Landon made her feel appreciated.

Jadin reached over and took his hand in her own. "Why don't we call it a night?" she suggested.

He moved his mouth over hers, kissing her hungrily. They made it as far as the living room floor.

Landon and Jadin spent Saturday at the children's festival Garland hosted annually. They were charged with watching Kai and Amya while Ryker spent some father-son time with R.J. at the event.

"Landon, will you help me with my castle?"

He smiled at Kai. "Sure."

Amya peered at them, then whispered, "Jadin, when did you get married? Was I there?"

"No, sweetie. Landon and I didn't have a big wedding like Austin and Bree, or Jordin and Ethan."

"I thought that was the only way you could get married."

Jadin chuckled. "No, there are different types of weddings."

"Oh," Amya responded as she colored the unicorn drawing. "When I get married, I'm going to have a wedding like Jordin's. I want a carriage and horses, too."

"I hope you're not planning on that anytime soon."

Amya giggled. "I'm too little to get married now, Jadin."

Amused, she responded, "Oh, I agree."

"I'm gonna make a picture for Emery since he couldn't come to the festival."

"That's so sweet," Jadin said. "He's gonna love it."

"Emery's sick," Kai contributed. "He has a fever."

Landon smiled, then placed a kiss on the little girl's forehead.

Jadin loved watching him with Kai and Amya. He

was so good with them. It was hard for anyone not to be, she told herself. The girls were so lovable.

Kai was the first to see Garland. "Hey, Mama."

"How's it going?" she asked Jadin.

"Don't worry. We're being good, Mommy," Amya responded. She never looked up from her coloring.

Jadin bit back a smile. "What she said."

"This festival is fantastic," Landon said.

"Thank you," Garland murmured. "I had a really good team this year." She checked her watch. "I need to make sure the storyteller is here."

"We're good," Jadin told her. "Landon and I will feed the girls, take them to get their faces painted and whatever else they want to do."

"Have you seen Ryker and R.J.?"

"They were making toy cars or something," Landon said. "They were over by the cotton candy stand about fifteen minutes ago."

"Thanks, I'll see if they're still there."

"This is a huge undertaking," Jadin said. "I'm always amazed at how Garland is able to pull something like this together."

At noon they got something to eat for the girls.

Afterward, Amya and Kai wanted to see the puppets. It was one of their favorite shows.

In the early July heat, Jadin's shirt clung to her skin. She was pleased with her decision to wear shorts instead of jeans.

Jadin headed straight to the shower when she and Landon arrived home. She looked over her shoulder at him and said, "Want to join me?" Her body ached for his touch.

Removing his clothes, Landon responded, "You don't have to ask me twice."

The next morning, Landon awoke to the delicious aroma of bacon frying. He showered, dressed and went down to the kitchen.

"Good morning," Jadin greeted.

He kissed her on the lips. "Need any help?"

She smiled at him. "No, thanks. I'm almost done."

Grinning, he asked, "When did you learn to make pancakes?"

Jadin gasped. "Are you really gonna go there? *Really?*"

Landon's hand was on her right hip, the searing touch of his fingers burning through her body like a brand.

"Hey, I'm just saying."

"Just because you can make perfectly round and pretty pancakes, you don't have to bash my misshapen ones."

Landon chuckled. "Baby, I don't care how your pancakes look. I'd eat them because I know they were made with love."

Jadin burst into laughter. "It's hard for me to argue with that."

She turned off the stove after the last stack of pancakes was ready. "These are by far my best-looking stack."

Landon cleaned up the kitchen when they finished breakfast.

"So, we're going to your uncle's house for dinner today?" he asked when he entered the master bedroom.

Jadin nodded. "Yes. Aunt Rochelle likes to do

themes. We might get an evening in Paris, or a journey through Italy... I don't know how she manages to come up with this stuff. It doesn't matter, though. The food is always good."

Landon laughed. "She's a very interesting person."

"Yes, she is." Jadin walked out of her closet with a black sundress. She stood in front of the full-length mirror, holding up the dress in front of her.

"You're going to look beautiful in whatever you put on."

She turned around, facing him. "Thank you."

Landon glanced over at the clock. "You know, we have a couple of hours before we have to leave."

Jadin quickly abandoned the dress, letting it fall to the floor, followed by her shorts and tank top.

# Chapter 13

"You okay?" Austin inquired.

"My stomach's upset. I had some chicken for lunch and I don't think it agreed with me." Jadin pointed to the folder in his hand. "What did the investigators find?"

"Sandra Davis worked a couple of flights to Los Angeles, but not on the night of Millicent's murder. She was supposed to work the flight to Chicago, but she switched with another attendant."

"Was she working the day of the funeral?"

"Nope. And get this—she rented cars on both days, here in Charleston."

"Austin, she's the one who stabbed Millicent. I'm sure of it."

"Does Landon know about Sandra?"

"If he does, he hasn't mentioned it."

"None of the prints match Sandra's," Austin said. "One more thing. Sandra Davis was once Sandra

Mayfield. She stabbed her husband after catching him in bed with another woman. She was charged with assault."

"I need to go see Blaine," Jadin said. "He needs to stay away from that woman."

"He needs to tell Landon about Sandra, too."

She still felt a little nauseous, but Jadin did not let that stop her from her task. Blaine was expecting her.

She pulled into the circular driveway and parked. Jadin stayed inside her car for another five minutes, willing her stomach to settle down.

Jadin made her way to the front door, which opened immediately.

"Come in," Blaine said.

They settled in the living room.

"Have you spoken to Sandra any more?" she asked.

"She's been calling to check on me," Blaine responded. "Why? What is this about? I told you I ended things with her."

"I wish there was another way to say this... Blaine, I believe she killed your wife."

Shaking his head, he uttered, "You're wrong."

"Sandra has been lying to you. She was in Charleston the night Millicent was killed. We have rental receipts to prove it. And I'm pretty sure she was the one who sent you the champagne."

"I can't believe she'd do something like this. Not Sandra."

"Blaine, she stabbed her ex-husband when she caught him with another woman. She's capable of violence."

"This is my fault," he said after a moment. "I brought that woman into our lives. I brought her to this house.

Milli's dead because of me." A lone tear rolled down his cheek.

"It's time for you to tell the police and Landon about her," Jadin said gently.

He nodded.

"I'll call the station to let them know that we're coming in."

Landon was at the police station when she and Blaine arrived. Jadin had notified him, as well.

"Is he about to confess?" Landon asked when they entered the observation room.

"No, but the truth is about to come out."

"I did not see that coming," Landon said. "But what real proof do we have that this woman sent the champagne and that she was the one who stabbed Millicent? It's pretty circumstantial."

"She was here in Charleston the night of the murder," Jadin told him. "Blaine thought he dreamed her up, but I'm sure it was actually a memory. She's no stranger to stabbing someone. Landon, my gut tells me that she killed Millicent because she knew Blaine would never leave her. She has more motive than anyone."

"She's coming to Charleston tonight, so the detectives will have a chance to interview her."

"Blaine had no problem convincing her to come," Jadin responded. "He's blaming himself for everything that happened."

"I can see why," Landon said. "It was his actions that set everything in motion. That's a heavy burden to carry."

"I need to take him back home." Jadin bent to retrieve her purse. Everything suddenly began spinning and then turned black.

* * *

"Wake up, Jadin. Can you hear me?" Landon said as he patted her cheek.

The deep voice came first, then Jadin's vision gradually started to clear.

"Oh, thank God. Are you all right?"

Her eyes followed the sound of the voice as she looked up, dazed. Trying hard to focus, she found herself staring into Landon's concerned brown eyes. "What happened?"

Jadin felt his hands on her arm and behind her back, helping her to rise.

"Take it easy, sweetheart. You fainted."

She rubbed her face with her hands. "Oh... I just remember getting dizzy suddenly. I think it's just the heat... I'm so sorry," Jadin blustered, brushing off her pants and avoiding Landon's gaze. Her heart skipped a beat at the worry she saw there.

Landon led her over to a nearby chair. "How are you feeling now?"

Jadin gripped the desk for support as she sat down. "Okay."

"We called for an ambulance," one of the detectives said.

"They don't need to come," Jadin interjected quickly. "I'm fine. Really."

"I think you still need to be checked out," Landon said.

Gratitude washed over her for his gallantry.

"The paramedics are here," someone announced.

They rushed to her side and checked her vitals.

Jadin could feel Landon's gaze on her. She looked

up and gave him a smile, hoping to remove the worry she saw in his expression.

"You're a little dehydrated," the paramedic named Greg told her.

"I'll drink lots of water," Jadin responded. "Thank you so much for coming. I feel like I've wasted your time, though."

"You haven't."

She was able to convince them that she did not need to go to the hospital.

"You've been working a lot of long hours," Landon said when the paramedics left. "And you haven't been feeling well for a couple of days. Maybe you should let me take you home."

"I'm good." Jadin stood up but rose too quickly. Her blood pressure dipped, and she saw black shapes behind her eyes once again.

His arms were instantly there to steady her. "Where are you going?" Landon's fingers were firm on her wrist as he helped her sit back down. "Stay put." He glanced over his shoulder. "Mike, can you take Herndon home?"

"Sure," the detective responded.

Jadin avoided his eyes. "Sorry about that."

"You don't need to apologize to me. Finish off your water," he said. "I'm taking you home. But first I'm going to get you something to eat."

He helped Jadin out to her car.

At home, Landon sent her straight to bed.

Settled against a stack of pillows, Jadin asked, "What are you going to do about your car?"

"I'll take an Uber back to the office." He pressed a

hand to her forehead. "You don't have a fever. Are you still feeling dizzy?"

"No, I'm actually feeling much better now. I was feeling nauseous earlier. I think the chicken I had for lunch didn't exactly agree with me."

"Do you think that had anything to do with your passing out?" he asked.

"I was just dehydrated, baby." She placed a hand to his cheek. "You don't have to worry about me. I'm fine."

"I'm always going to worry about the woman I love. You know, I don't have to go back to the office," Landon offered. "I can work from home."

"I really would rather not be alone."

"Then you don't have to be." He loosened his tie, then climbed into bed with her.

"I should probably check on Blaine."

"Honey, he was there when you passed out. He will be fine. His girlfriend... That's another story."

Jadin snuggled against him. "Looks like we may each come out of this with a victory." Her eyes drifted shut.

Landon peered over at her.

She was sound asleep.

He eased out of bed and went into the guest room to get some work done while Jadin was sleeping.

Two hours passed, and Landon navigated to the kitchen to start on dinner. He decided against chicken since she had had that earlier. He placed a quick call to Aubrie.

"Hey, Jadin's not feeling well and I'm trying to think of something she can eat."

"Is she nauseous?"

"Some, but she passed out earlier. She was dehydrated."

"I'll bring over a tomato-eggplant-zucchini casserole. I made some for Bree and there's enough left to drop a dish off to you and Jadin, as well."

"I was just calling to get some suggestions on what to cook, but this is even better. Thank you."

"We're family," Aubrie said. "We have to look out for one another. I also have a delicious grapefruit-and-blackberry fruit salad. I'll bring that, too. All of this will help with dehydration."

"Thank you again."

"I'll see you in about ten minutes. I was just about to leave the house when you called."

Landon released a long sigh of relief.

Jadin felt rested after her two-hour nap. She had been more tired than usual lately.

She turned on the television in time to catch the unfolding story of Sandra's confession and arrest. It was the topic among Charleston's most prominent social circles. Many were shocked by the news that Blaine Herndon had been involved with that woman. Loyalties were divided because his affair had caused Millicent's death.

Landon must be working, she decided when she opened her eyes and saw that she was in the room alone.

She sat up in bed when she heard voices.

A knock sounded, and the door opened. Aubrie stuck her head inside. "Hey, just wanted to see how you're doing. You gave your hubby quite a scare."

"I feel so much better," Jadin said.

"Well, I dropped off some food for you two. Make sure you eat."

"Oh, I will," she promised. "I've never been so embarrassed, passing out like that. In the police station of all places."

"Looks like you won your case. Your client was innocent."

Jadin nodded. "I'm happy that it wasn't at Landon's expense. I know that there are going to be other cases where we're going to bump heads, but I'm relieved that it's not this case. Our marriage is still very fragile."

"I think you and Landon are going to be fine. I haven't known him very long, but I can see how much he cares for you. The poor man called me for advice on what to feed you."

Smiling, Jadin said, "Did he really?"

Aubrie nodded. "That's why I'm here. I brought dinner."

She hugged her cousin. "Thank you for being such a sweetheart."

"Girl, you know how we do." Aubrie scanned her face. "You look really happy, Jadin."

"I am," she responded. "Landon's always been a good man, but he's turning out to be a great husband. Sometimes I pinch myself just to be sure I'm not dreaming."

"I take it that you didn't feel this way about Michael."

"Michael and I had some good times, Aubrie. He was good to me, but what I've realized is that I wasn't myself with him the way I am with Landon. He isn't very close to his family and he thinks I spend too much with mine… I'm not sure it would've really worked out between us."

"I'm really happy for you, Jadin."

"What about you, Aubrie? I know you're not always cooking when you go to New Orleans. Who is he?"

"I'm not ready to say. I don't want to jinx it."

"I knew it. I knew there was someone special in your life."

"All I'm gonna say is that he is a strong possibility," Aubrie said. "And he's very handsome."

"Well, I can't wait to meet him."

"I hate to interrupt," Landon said when he entered the bedroom, carrying a tray of food, "but you need to eat something."

"He's right," Aubrie said.

"Okay, you two don't need to gang up on me."

Standing up, Aubrie said, "I have to go. I need to drop off some food to Bree and Austin."

"Thank you," Jadin and Landon said in unison.

He walked Aubrie downstairs while Jadin attacked the casserole. All of a sudden, Jadin felt ravenous.

## Chapter 14

Ryker whisked Garland off for a romantic weekend, so Jadin and Landon volunteered to babysit the children.

"They are all finally asleep," Jadin said as she sat down beside him.

Landon chuckled. "How many times did you have to read that story to them?"

"Four."

He handed her a cup of hot peppermint tea. "I have to admit that it feels nice hearing the sound of children playing in this house."

She nodded in agreement. "It does."

Jadin took a sip of her tea. "They really adore you."

"I'm crazy about them, too. That little R.J. is a talker. I just wish I knew what he was saying."

They laughed.

Jadin glanced around the room, the lighting a warm,

flattering shade of gold against the muted mustard-colored walls. She settled back against the luxuriously soft couch with a throw pillow on her lap. She leaned against Landon. "I don't know about you, but I'm exhausted."

Landon wrapped an arm around her. "You've been tired a lot lately. I'm glad Sandra confessed to everything...the drugging and the stabbing. We can finally close that case. Now you can cut back on some of those late hours."

"Hopefully." She stifled a yawn. "I'm sorry, baby."

He kissed her on the cheek. "Go on up to bed. I'll be there shortly. I'm going to check on the little ones, then I'll join you."

"I love you, Landon."

He smiled. "I love you, too."

On Tuesday, Jadin left the doctor's office in a daze. She lay her hand over her still perfectly flat abdomen.

*I'm pregnant.*

For her, it was wonderful news. She and Landon had not really discussed starting a family. The day before he moved in, Jadin had seen her doctor and had her birth control changed because of the side effects.

Her doctor had explained that when she switched birth control pills, her body needed time to adjust to the new hormones. She told Jadin that by switching to the new birth control, it was like starting for the first time.

Jadin vaguely recalled Dr. Stevens recommending that she use an alternative form of protection for a month, while her body adjusted to the new birth control pills.

She had not used any other form of contraceptive, and now she was going to have a baby.

Not ready to go back to the office just yet, Jadin drove to see her sister.

"Hey, how are you feeling?" Jordin asked. "Dad said you passed out at the police station."

"I'm fine."

"Really?"

Jadin nodded. "I just left the doctor's office. I'm pregnant."

"I thought you were on the Pill."

"I had them switched the day before Landon moved in. I forgot all about Dr. Stevens telling me to use another form of protection for a month."

"You were dealing with a lot" Jordin murmured. "Landon will make a great father."

"I think so, too."

"Then what's wrong, sis?"

"I guess I'm still in shock."

"Do you love him?"

Jadin nodded. "I do."

"He loves you, too. This baby you're carrying was conceived out of love. Everything is going to be fine. Landon's gonna love being a father. I've seen the way he is with the kids."

"He's great with all of them, including these two little muffins," she murmured, as she looked down at the sleeping twins.

"Aren't you glad you stayed with him?"

"Jordin, this was the best decision I've ever made. It's almost like we never were apart all those years."

"You seem to be a lot happier now."

"I am," she confirmed. "I feel so comfortable with Landon. We have so much fun together."

"What about Michael?"

Jadin looked at her sister. "It's over between us. I don't think that he and I would have really worked in the long term."

"I see you more with Landon than with Michael."

Jadin chose a designer navy pantsuit to wear for her meeting with a new client at the Belmond Charleston Place. She was about to head back to her office when she heard her name called.

"Jadin…"

She turned around. "Michael, what are you doing here?" She had not expected to see him anytime soon, if ever.

"I'm staying here. I came in last night. I didn't want to go by the house. I figured Landon moved in already."

"What are you doing in town?"

"It should be obvious," he responded with a smile. "I came to see you. Can we go somewhere and talk?"

"I don't think we have anything to discuss," she said.

"Please, Jadin."

"Sure."

"I'll drive," Michael said.

"I'm still not understanding why you're in town. Are you here for business?"

"Jadin, I came here specifically to see you, but figured I'd check out the competition while in town."

Now she understood why he had stayed at the Belmond and not the Alexander-DePaul Hotel. "I'm really surprised to see you, Michael. The way we left things—I figured I'd never hear from you again."

He drove to Battery Park.

They strolled along the waterfront.

"How are things going between you and Landon?" Michael inquired.

"They're good," she responded. "No complaints."

"I have to admit that I didn't think you'd last this long. I figured you'd be calling and begging me to take you back, but the call never came." He shook his head. "I don't understand how you can continue in this farce of a marriage."

"I made a commitment to give it a year." Jadin could not believe Michael had the nerve to think she'd ever beg him for anything. It was clear that he did not really know her at all. "But even if things had ended between me and Landon, I'd never come to you *begging* for anything."

"You don't want to be with him." Michael scoffed. "Why don't you just end this now? Jadin, get your divorce so we can move on with our lives as husband and wife. I hired one of the top divorce attorneys in South Carolina."

Jadin looked up at him. "What gives you the right to do something like that?"

"I've had some time to think about everything. I never should have encouraged you to stay in this sham of a marriage. I let my emotions get the best of me."

"There's something you don't seem to understand," she said. "This is completely *my* decision, Michael."

"You never would have decided this if I'd stayed here."

The man was delusional.

Jadin held her temper in check. "Michael, I'm not

going to divorce Landon," she told him. "Our marriage is real. I love him."

He chuckled. "No, you don't. Just a few months ago, you were going to be my wife. I know that you're just confused. I told you that you can be too emotional at times. I know what it is about Landon. He's probably the mushy type. He leaves little notes or serves you breakfast in bed and brings home flowers. Babe, that stuff doesn't make a relationship."

"What do you think makes the relationship, Michael?"

"We're a good team, Jadin. We don't need all that stuff. We will have loads of money. We can do whatever we want. We can travel around the world..."

"What about children?"

"What about them?" Michael asked. "The world has enough rug rats running all over the place. We don't need to add to them."

Frowning, Jordin inquired, "You don't want children?"

"No, I don't. I had enough of them with your little cousins. Seems like every time I turn around, one of my cousins is having a baby. People like the Alexanders and DuGrandpres put a lot of stock into lineage." He bent down and kissed her. "Babe, all we need is each other."

Jadin rolled her eyes as she pushed his hand away. "Don't do that again," she uttered, resisting the urge to slap him in public. "Michael, the last thing I ever want to do is hurt you, but the truth is that Landon and I belong together. We're in sync. With you, I was the one who always had to compromise—that's not how a relationship is supposed to work."

"Jadin..."

"No, Michael," she said, cutting him off. "I'm choosing Landon. I want the life I have with him. He and I want the same things, including a family. You and I never would have worked out."

"That's not true. We had a great relationship for three years."

"No, we didn't," Jadin said. "I just didn't complain or make waves. I did a lot of settling—something I won't ever do again." She checked her watch. "I need to get back to my car."

"Babe…"

"Don't call me that," Jadin stated. "You know what? I'll take an Uber back."

"You don't have to do that," Michael responded. "Let's go."

# Chapter 15

Landon enjoyed the incredible views of Fort Sumter and the Sullivan's Island Lighthouse from Battery Park, which was why he often came here to eat his lunch. He found an empty spot near the gazebo.

His eyes traveled to the couple walking along the waterfront. Landon could not believe what he was seeing.

*Jadin and Michael.*

Something grabbed at his chest like a sharp talon. Its grip tightened and squeezed.

Landon nearly lost it when Michael kissed her.

His chest gave another suffocating spasm. The sight of them kissing made his insides feel hollow and empty, as if they had been scraped out with something sharp. It took every fiber of his being not to go over and confront them.

*This is not the time or place*, he told himself.

The atmosphere around him had suddenly become shaming. Embarrassing. Excruciating.

Landon knew it was foolish to dream. Foolish to hope. Foolish to fall in love with someone who was so far out of his reach. But he had always loved Jadin. He could not remember a time when he had not loved her.

There was a time when she had returned that love, but from the looks of it, Jadin had made her decision and Landon decided to do the same.

His chest seized again as Landon tried to ignore the sinking sensation in the pit of his stomach.

Instead of going back to the office, Landon drove to the gym, where he worked off some, but not all, of his unsettled feelings. He ran twelve miles on the treadmill. Pushed a few weights around. Did a hundred abdominal crunches, and yet he still could not get the image of Jadin and Michael kissing out of his mind. He was angry with himself mostly. He had been selfish and now he was paying the price for that selfishness.

He went home, showered and put on trousers, a shirt and a tie. Landon grabbed a blazer and headed back to the office. He intended to make it a late night.

Jadin decided she would not tell Landon about Michael's little visit. Things were going well between them and she had more important news to share with him. She pressed her hand to her stomach. "I love you already," she whispered. "I can't wait to tell your daddy about you."

She made his favorite, beef Stroganoff, for dinner. Jadin lit the candles in the dining room, then ran upstairs to slip into something a little sexier.

Thirty minutes passed.

Jadin checked the clock, then called Landon.

When the call went to voice mail, she left a message. "Hey, I expected you home a half hour ago. Can you give me a call back just to let me know that you're okay? I made beef Stroganoff for you. Call me, please."

Landon called her five minutes later.

"I'm sorry for not calling you to let you now that I'm working late," he said. "It's been a crazy day for me."

Jadin tried to keep her disappointment from her voice. "Any idea when you'll be home? I really need to talk to you."

"It's going to be a late night," Landon responded.

"Like how late?"

"I'm not sure, Jadin. All I can say is that you shouldn't wait up for me."

"Are you okay?" she asked. Landon did not sound like himself. In fact, Jadin got the distinct impression that he was upset about something.

"I'm just busy."

"Okay. Well, I guess I'll let you get back to work, then." Jadin ended the call.

She put away the food, blew out the candles and went upstairs to her bedroom.

Jadin changed into a pair of pajamas, then climbed into bed. "I guess your daddy is too busy for us tonight."

The thought that something was going on with Landon still nagged at her. She considered calling him back but changed her mind. Jadin really did not want to disturb him at work.

She stole a peek at the clock on the nightstand.

Jadin decided to do some reading. She hoped Landon would end up surprising her by coming home early.

Before she felt asleep, Jadin sent him a text.

Don't work too hard. I miss you.

She did not get a response.

Landon glanced down at the text, but chose not to respond, but only because he did not know what to say at this point.

He already knew what she wanted to discuss. She wanted to tell him that she wanted to be with Michael. His stomach clenched as if a fist had grabbed at his intestines.

At the moment, Landon's heart could not take hearing those words come out of her mouth, so he avoided going home until he felt Jadin had fallen asleep.

He slept in the guest room.

The next morning, Landon was up early. He showered, dressed and left before seven o'clock.

Landon was busy going through case law when a young woman appeared at his office door. "Good morning, Landon."

He looked up to find Janice, the newest prosecutor standing there. "Morning," he greeted in return.

She walked into his office and sat down. "I want to say thank you for all your help."

"It's no problem."

"I'd like to buy you dinner to show my appreciation."

He smiled. "Janice, you don't have to do that." Something about the way she was eyeing him made Landon wary.

"But I want to," she insisted. "I noticed you're the last one to leave and the first to arrive—you're so dedicated. As you know, my father is a federal prosecutor. I really want to make him proud, so I'd like for you to be my mentor."

"I've only been on this job a brief time," Landon said. "I think you should ask Trudy Mims to be your mentor."

"I would rather have you as a mentor. I feel like we have a real connection." She gave a short chuckle. "I didn't mean it the way that sounded."

Landon did not respond.

"Will you at least consider it?"

"I'll think about it."

Solicitous.

That was the only way Jadin could describe Landon's behavior toward her over the past two days. He was very polite…solicitous. Jadin still could not escape the feeling that something was wrong.

"You've been working some long hours," she told him when he came downstairs.

"I have a lot going on right now. It's this case I'm working on and I have this new prosecutor that's shadowing me."

"I made some coffee."

"Thank you." He gave her a polite smile and poured himself a cup of coffee.

"Landon, why have you been sleeping in the guest room?"

"I get in so late. I don't want to disturb you."

"I've missed you. To be honest, I feel like there's something going on between us."

He looked at her. "What could be wrong?"

"I don't know," Jadin responded with a slight shrug. "But I feel like there's some tension between us. There's something I've been wanting to tell you…"

Landon glanced at his watch. "I need to get out of here. I'm gonna grab something to eat on the way to work."

"Will you be home for dinner?"

"Probably not," Landon replied.

"Can't you do some of your work at home?" Jadin asked. "I really need to talk to you."

He shook his head. "I'm working this case with another prosecutor."

She stepped in front of him, blocking his exit. "Don't I get a kiss, fist bump…something?"

Landon kissed her cheek. "I'll try to make it home before you go to bed. We can talk then."

Jadin moved over to the counter to inspect the floral arrangement rather than let him see how much his response disappointed her.

Landon knew he could not avoid Jadin for much longer. It was only delaying the inevitable. He knew she wanted out of the marriage. Despite all they had shared, she still wanted Michael. The sting of betrayal was like a poison spreading throughout his body.

Tonight, he would come home, and they would have their talk. He would give her what she wanted—a divorce.

"I never should have come here," he whispered. *I should have just filed those papers years ago.* What angered him most was her ability to lie to him so easily. Landon had never known her to be such a skilled liar. This was all an elaborate scheme to pay him back for keeping their marriage a secret from her.

"Good morning," Janice greeted when he came through the doors of the prosecutor's office. She was sitting at one of the tables with the receptionist in the break room.

He returned the greeting, then headed straight to his office.

Five minutes later, Janice knocked on his open door. "I know why I'm here, but what brings you in so early?"

"I wanted to get a head start on some work."

"Is this what I can expect?"

Landon looked up from his computer monitor. "Excuse me?"

"Working all these long hours," Janice said, "I just want to know what I've gotten myself into."

"There are times when a case might call for it, but it's not really the norm unless you're not organized or good with time management." Landon smiled. "Janice, I think you'll do fine."

She flashed him a sexy grin.

Landon was by no means blinded to her attraction to him, and although she was young and beautiful, he was not interested in her. He maintained a professional distance.

He spent most of his morning going over a hit-and-run accident, a statutory rape case and an incident involving elder abuse in a local nursing home.

Landon worked through lunch on the case he was working with another prosecutor.

It was another high-profile case involving a hip-hop artist.

Before he realized it, six o'clock had come and gone.

"I had a feeling you'd still be here," Janice said. "I really admire your dedication."

Landon leaned back in his chair. "Why are you still here?"

"I was shadowing Trudy." She sauntered into his office. "I'm about to grab something to eat. Why don't you join me?"

His stomach growled loudly.

Landon was not ready to go home just yet, so he said, "Sure."

"Great," Janice responded. "And I'm buying dinner. This is my way of saying thank you." As if she knew what he was thinking, she added, "I invited Trudy, but she has a date with her fiancé."

When they neared the elevator, Janice said, "Landon, I have a confession to make. I hate eating alone."

"What about your friends? This is your home, right?"

"I don't really have a lot of people in my inner circle," she responded.

"I find that hard to believe."

Janice smiled. "Why do you say that?"

"You seem like a people person," Landon said.

They walked across the street to the restaurant on the corner.

"I love people," Janice said, "but I don't do drama. Some of my friends have nothing but, so I had to make some changes. They're still my girls, but I can't have their drama messing up what I'm trying to do."

"I can understand that."

After they were seated, Janice asked, "So, what is it like being married to a DuGrandpre?"

"I suppose it's like any other marriage," he responded.

"I haven't met your wife, but I've been around her twin, Jordin. I have a membership to Ethan's gym, so I see her there from time to time." Janice picked up her menu. "She seems really nice."

"She is," Landon confirmed.

"I can't imagine being married to a defense attorney. Seems like there would be some sort of conflict of interest."

"There isn't as long as everyone involved with the case is informed of the relationship. However, Jadin and I have agreed that we would not work the same cases anymore." Landon eyed his menu.

"I was following the Herndon case. Millicent and my mother were friends. We were all shocked that Blaine had cheated on her. He just never was that type of man."

"I'm glad the truth came out. I never want to send an innocent man to prison or worse."

Janice laid her menu down. "Landon, I have a feeling that even though you're sitting here with me, you're not really here. Are you okay?"

"I am," he replied. "I'm just tired."

The server came to take their orders.

She studied him openly. "No, you're not just tired. There's something more going on with you. It's okay if you don't want to talk about it."

"I don't."

Janice shrugged in nonchalance. "That's fine with me."

Landon glanced down at the wedding band on his left hand. After tonight, there would be no need to wear it anymore.

# Chapter 16

Jadin decided to grab dinner out. Since Landon was not going to be home, she wasn't in the mood for cooking.

She was surprised to walk into Leonardo's and see Landon with a young, beautiful woman. They were talking and laughing, oblivious to everyone around them. Her heart felt as if someone had just plunged a knife through it.

Tears filled her eyes, prompting Jadin to blink rapidly. She refused to let them spill down her cheeks. She refused to break down and cry in public.

She turned around and walked out of the restaurant.

Unable to control her tears any longer, Jadin wiped her face with the backs of her hands as she made her way to her car.

"Working late my…"

She regained her composure and made it home.

Landon arrived home an hour later.

"I thought you were working," Jadin said dryly.

"You told me that you needed to talk to me, so I'm here."

"Now you're suddenly interested in what I have to say?"

He seemed taken aback by her words. "Jadin, I needed to think some things over, but now I'm ready to talk. But I'd like to go first."

"Okay."

"When I walked back into your life four months ago, you were blindsided. You had moved on with another man, but I pushed you to stay in our marriage. I realize now that I was wrong."

"Excuse me?"

"I never should have forced you to stay with me, Jadin. That's not the way real love works. It wasn't fair to you."

"What are you saying, Landon?"

"This is my gift to you." He handed her divorce papers. "I've signed them."

Stunned, Jadin did not know how to respond. Her eyes filled with tears. "This is what you want?"

"This is for the best."

"What's the rush, Landon? Would this have something to do with a certain young woman you were having dinner with earlier?"

His eyes registered his surprise.

"Is she the *prosecutor* you've been spending all this time with?" She wiped away her tears. "You know what? It doesn't matter. You've made up your mind." Jadin held up the papers. "This time I'll make sure these are filed."

"I don't doubt that you will," Landon responded. "I hope you and Michael will be very happy together."

She could tell he was angry. He was just too polite to show it. Jadin was too caught up in her emotions to comprehend exactly why Landon was so upset.

"I never thought you could be such a jerk. *Get out of my house, now.*"

She rushed into her office and broke down into sobs. Landon had never been one to be cruel and unfeeling. He did not even bother to deny that he was having an intimate dinner with another woman. He did not bother to explain why he was with her. He simply handed her divorce papers and wished her luck with Michael.

*Who does that?*

At least he offered to divorce her instead of going behind her back with another woman all over Charleston. Still, she had never felt so betrayed in her life.

She stayed in her office until Landon knocked on the door.

"I'm leaving," he said. "I left the keys and the garage opener on the counter in the kitchen." Landon paused a moment, then said, "I'm sorry about this, Jadin."

"I don't want your apologies. I don't want anything from you except you out of my house."

"That's fine, because I can't live with the ghost of another person between us."

"Now you don't have to worry about that," Jadin uttered in response.

Tears filled her eyes at the reality that she was losing her husband and the father of her child—the child Landon had no knowledge existed. Instinctively, her hands went to her stomach. "I'm so sorry, little one. I love your daddy so much, but I can't hold on to him when he doesn't want to be here with us. Now, don't you worry... When I tell him about you, he's going to be so happy. I can't tell him right now because he'll only stay with me because of you. I don't want that for myself."

Jadin felt like she wanted to die. Right now, she wanted the ground to open, swallow her whole and spit her out on the other side of the world.

Jordin stuck her head inside her sister's office. "Hey... you have lunch plans?"

Jadin was surprised to see her twin. She wasn't due back for another couple of weeks. "What are you doing here?"

"I needed to pick up some files." Jordin eyed her. "What's wrong?"

"He's gone."

Closing the door behind her, Jordin asked, "What do you mean by he's gone?"

"Landon's *gone*." She held out the divorce papers. "This is his gift to me."

"This doesn't make sense at all."

"It makes perfect sense to me," Jadin said. "He doesn't want to be my husband any longer. He's been very distant, claimed he's been working late, and when he did come home, he would sleep in the guest room. Then last night, I saw him with another woman, having dinner when he was supposed to working."

"There's got to be more to it than that, sis. Dinner doesn't mean that he's having an affair. She was probably his coworker. You know we do it all the time when we're working on a complicated case. Late hours... grabbing dinner together, then back to work."

"Landon wouldn't be leaving me unless he really cares for that woman."

"Did you tell him about the baby?"

"I don't want him staying with me just because of a child. It's better that he doesn't know for now. I'll wait until the divorce is final."

"Jadin, I don't think that's a good idea."

"Landon left me no choice, Jordin." She burst into sobs.

"You have to tell him that you're pregnant, sis. He deserves to know—you don't have to take him back, but he should know."

"I'm not going to keep it from him. I'm just not telling him right now." Jadin wiped her face with a tissue. "Right now, I can only deal with one thing at a time."

"Are you really going through with this divorce?"

She nodded. "It's what Landon wants."

"I don't think so," Jordin said. "He loves you. I know it."

"I thought he did, too."

"Are you sure nothing else happened?"

"It has to do with that woman I saw him with," Jadin said. "I'm sure of it. His timing is something else. I'm pregnant and Michael came to town a few days ago to tell me that he wanted me back."

"Really?"

"Yeah, but I told him that I was in love with Landon and I was staying in my marriage."

"Huh…that's interesting."

"What?"

"Landon starts acting strange during the same time that you run into Michael."

"He doesn't know anything about Michael's visit.

I never mentioned it to him, because that's when he suddenly had to work late. Besides, Landon would've said something about it."

"I don't think you should give up on your marriage. If you want Landon, fight for him. You know what I had to deal with when Ethan and I were dating. Remember, I ended our engagement, but we were able to work through our issues."

"Jordin, he handed me a signed divorce petition. Just like I gave him five years ago. This is payback. I really believe it."

"Landon is not petty like that."

"The marriage is over, and I accept it."

"Do me a favor and hold off on filing those papers."

"Why?"

"Because it's not what either of you really want. There's a missing piece of this puzzle and you shouldn't do anything until you have all of the pieces together."

"I'll think about it, Jordin."

# Chapter 17

"Son, I think you just made the biggest mistake of your life," Tim Trent told his nephew. "Then you letting her think you're seeing another woman…"

"Why do you say that?" Landon asked. "She's still in love with Michael. Let her see how it feels to be betrayed."

"I have another suggestion. How about being a grown-up and confronting your wife about what you saw?"

"No, Uncle… What's the point? All this time she's been trying to convince herself that she wanted me, but her heart belongs to Michael."

"What if you're wrong about what you saw? What if it wasn't the way it looked? Everything is not always as it seems. You know that, Landon. Look at what she thought when she saw you with that other woman. You were having dinner with a coworker."

"She and Michael were kissing."

"You saw that man kiss your wife. At least that's what you told me."

"Jadin didn't look as if she minded."

"Were they all wrapped up? Her arms around his neck?"

"No, but she didn't slap him or run off like she was angry with him, either."

"Landon, I think you need to talk to her. If you don't, you're gonna regret this for the rest of your life."

He considered his uncle's words. Perhaps he was making more out of this than it really was. If he had just confronted them together, he would not be in such torment now. "Maybe you're right. I should go talk to Jadin."

"Now you're thinking," his uncle said. "This is not the time for you to go rushing off into divorce court."

"Austin...hey..." Jadin stepped aside to let her brother enter the house the next day. She'd decided to take a day off. She did not want to face everyone with her face swollen from crying all night. "I know you talked to Jordin. You didn't have to come over here. I'm fine."

"I'm not understanding what's going on with you two. Where's Landon? I need to talk to him."

"He's not here, Austin. Don't waste your time. If Landon wants a divorce, I'm going to give him one."

They settled down in the family room.

"Now I know how he must have felt when I did this to him," Jadin said. "I keep thinking that maybe that's what this is all about—Landon wanted me to feel how much this hurts."

"Do you really believe that?" Austin asked.

Jadin shook her head. "It's the only thing that makes sense. I thought everything was good between us, but I guess I was wrong." She wiped away a tear. "His timing really sucks, too."

"Why do you say that?"

"I'm pregnant, Austin."

"Does Landon know?"

Jadin shook her head no. "I didn't get a chance to tell him."

"You can't keep this a secret. It's not fair to keep Landon in the dark."

"I know what Jasmine put you through, Austin, but this is different. I don't want him to feel obligated to stay in our marriage just because of this baby. I know Landon, and he'll do just that—he'd stay with me."

Jadin wiped away her tears.

Austin embraced her. "I'm so sorry."

"I'll be okay. I just need to cry this out, but then I'll be fine."

"Are you sure?" he asked. "I need to check on Bree. She's already dilated two centimeters."

"You go be with her. I'm good."

"She's not in labor or anything. I just want to be home with her in case the contractions start. Bree's a little nervous about the whole labor and delivery."

"Call me when she does go to the hospital. I want to be there for her."

"I will."

Ten minutes after Austin left, Jadin was about to go upstairs when the doorbell sounded.

She opened the door to find Michael standing there. "What are you doing here?"

"I came here in the hopes of talking some sense into you. I know Landon's at work, so I figured we could talk."

Jadin glared at him. "You couldn't be more wrong."

His smile vanished. "What?"

"I thought I'd made myself pretty clear," Jadin uttered. "I love Landon. I'm sorry, Michael, but this is the truth." She burst into tears.

"Why are you crying?"

"Because Landon wants out." Jadin placed a hand to her stomach. "I don't know what happened. Everything was fine…"

Michael's eyes traveled downward. "Are you pregnant?"

Jadin followed his gaze. "Yes."

"Is this why you want to stay in this marriage? Because you got knocked up?"

"I want to stay in my marriage because I love my husband, Michael. It's that simple."

"Even though he doesn't want you."

"You can be such a jerk sometimes."

"What? You want me to be sympathetic?" Michael asked. "You left me for a man who has decided he doesn't want to be with you."

"Get out."

"You know, I was willing to take you back, but now that you're pregnant…"

"I would never go back to the miserable life I had with you," Jadin screamed. "You are insensitive, unyielding and a user. You have an uncle and a host of cousins who all love you and want to be a part of your life—you only have need of them when you need money or a cushy job. I love my family, and the whole time I was with you, I had to do a lot of compromising and sacrificing. That's not love, Michael."

"I don't care what you think of me," he responded. "You didn't live my life. You don't know what I've been through, so you don't get the right to tell me how to be or how to treat my family—family who think they're doing me a favor by handing me a dollar or two."

"They are not like that at all. Remember, I've met them, Michael. Malcolm and Barbara Alexander have been wonderful to you. You're just ungrateful."

"Instead of trying to be my shrink, why don't you figure out what you've done to run away your husband? Heck, for all I know, he's done me a favor."

*"He certainly did me a favor,"* Jadin responded. "He saved me from making what would have been a terrible mistake."

Without a word, Michael turned and walked out the front door.

# *Chapter 18*

Landon sat in his SUV, watching as Michael got into his car and drove away. He had seen enough to know that he'd made the right decision. He turned the ignition and pulled out.

Twenty minutes later, Landon walked into the chic foyer of the hotel. Crystal chandeliers overhead threw bright prisms of light over the polished marble floor. The late-summer air was filled with the scent of fresh peonies and roses and lilies from a giant and artfully arranged bouquet in the center of the area. Any other time, he would relish the sweet aroma, but today it made him sick to his stomach.

The lobby was buzzing with activity as people checked in and out. Landon quickly made his way to the elevator. He just wanted to escape to the empty silence of his suite.

Once there, he just sat on the sofa, staring into space.

The thought that Michael had spent the night with Jadin crossed his mind, but he chased it away as swiftly as it had come. He could not handle the idea of someone touching the woman who was still his wife, even if she did not act like it.

As much as Landon wanted to blame Jadin, he could not. He set this in motion when he selfishly refused to file those papers five years ago.

*I should've let her go then.*

If he had done what Jadin had asked of him back then, they would not be in this space today. This was his fault, Landon reasoned. *I brought this on myself.*

He thought once more on his uncle's words, but it was hard for him to accept that there was nothing going on between Jadin and Michael. This was the second time he had seen them together.

He considered himself a smart man, and he trusted his instincts. He saw Jadin and Michael together, but did that mean that there was something between them?

Landon thought back to Blaine Herndon and how he had believed the man to be guilty of murdering his wife, although there had been no concrete evidence.

*What if I'm wrong about Jadin?*

Austin and Bree welcomed a six-pound ten-ounce baby girl on Friday morning.

Jadin had spent the night at the hospital with her parents and Austin's mother, Irene.

"Why don't you go home?" Eleanor suggested. "You look so tired."

She had walked into her relationship with Landon with her heart wide-open and he had shattered it like broken glass. Jadin took deep breaths until she was strong enough to raise her head. "I'll leave in a few, but I need to talk to you, Mom."

"Okay, would you like to get some tea?"

Jadin nodded.

They walked down to the cafeteria.

"What's going on, hon?"

Tears slowly found their way down her cheeks. "Landon and I are getting a divorce."

Eleanor looked stunned by the news. "But why?"

"He doesn't want to stay in the marriage," she responded, wiping her face with a tissue found in her pocket. "Landon signed a divorce petition a few days ago. He wants out."

Her mother's expression was one of puzzlement. "What happened?"

"I don't know, Mom... I don't know." Jadin did not want to mention that another woman might be involved. At least not just yet. She also did not say anything about the baby. "Maybe I'm just destined to be a single woman, stuffing my face with seafood and white chocolate, and watching *Law & Order* throughout the night or reading on my Kindle."

"This just doesn't make any sense," Eleanor said. "It's clear how much that man loves you, Jadin. And I know that you love him, too. You two should seek counseling or something. Divorce should never be a choice when two people love one another."

"I agree," Jadin said. "But I will not force a man to stay with me when he doesn't want to be there."

"Does he know that you're pregnant?" Eleanor inquired.

Jadin gasped. "How did you find out?"

"Sweetie, you're my daughter. I just don't understand

why you haven't said anything to me. What's with all the secrets?"

"Mom, please don't be hurt. I didn't say anything because I don't want you thinking badly of Landon. He doesn't know about the baby. I didn't tell him because I know he'd stay. I want him to *choose* me. Not stay in a marriage because he's obligated."

"So, it's better that you take this decision away from him? Do you really think this is right?"

"I don't know."

"It appears to me that you two make decisions and think they should be law." Eleanor reached over and took her daughter's hand in her own. "You need to pray about this, Jadin. Because what you and Landon are doing is making a mockery of marriage. Either you two are going to be married or you're not, but you both need to be on the same page."

Jadin swallowed hard and bit back tears. "Mom, I want my marriage. Landon is the one who changed his mind. I wasn't going to say anything about this, but I think he's met someone else. He was supposed to be working late but I saw him at a restaurant with another woman."

"What did he say?"

"Nothing really."

"They recently hired a new prosecutor," Eleanor said. "You know your father used to take all of the new associates to dinner. I was out a couple of times and ran into him dining with some pretty girl."

"It never bothered you?"

"If I chose to believe the worse, of course it would bother me, but I refused to let my mind go there."

"You think I made a rush to judgment."

Eleanor nodded. "I do."

"So, what do I do now?"

"Go away for the weekend. That seems to always help to clear your head."

Jadin gave a small smile. "I'll drive down to Jekyll Island."

"It'll do you some good."

"Mom, I think you're right."

Eleanor embraced her. "You and Landon belong together. I knew it the moment I met the man…and got over my shock that you'd already married him. This is just a bump in the road, sweetie. I really believe that you two can overcome anything."

Jadin left the hospital and went home to pack.

She slept for a few hours before making the three-and-a-half-hour drive to Jekyll Island.

When she arrived, she settled down in her hotel suite, then ordered room service. Jadin did not feel like being around a lot of people.

She took a sip of bottled water as she stood on the balcony of her room, gazing at the beauty of the sandy stretch of beach below and the greenish color of the ocean. It reminded her of a conversation she had had with Landon.

They were discussing whether the Pacific and Atlantic Oceans were different colors. Jadin thought the Pacific Ocean was blue, while the Atlantic was more of a greenish color. Landon's theory was the two oceans were the same color.

A smiled tugged at her lips as she recalled them sitting side by side on laptop computers, looking for answers.

*"It depends on the day for the color of the ocean,"*

Landon told her. *"According to this website, the color is dependent on several factors. The deepest parts of the ocean will look blue because of the way the light is absorbed and reflected."*

*"Every time I go down to Jekyll Island, the ocean looks green to me,"* she responded.

*"I've seen it look lighter near the coast and like a deep sapphire color several miles from shore,"* Landon said. *"From what I've read, if there's a storm that's kicked up dirt, those particles can also change how light is absorbed in the water."*

*Jadin burst into laughter. "Can you believe we're actually sitting here, discussing the color of the ocean?"*

*He had leaned over, kissing her. "Of course. We're interested in stuff like this. There's nothing wrong with it—we just have a natural curiosity about things."*

A tear rolled down her check as Jadin considered there would never been any more of those moments with Landon.

She was glad to be away from Charleston. If Jadin had her way, she would just stay to hide away for a while. She lingered on the balcony, inhaling the ocean scent and the cool breeze.

She had no appetite but forced herself to eat. She had the baby to consider and she wanted him or her to be healthy.

Jordin called to check on her.

"I'm fine," she assured her sister. "I came to Jekyll Island to think things over."

"Mom told me. I'm glad to hear that you're at least considering fighting for your marriage."

"I'm going to sort out everything. But it's not really up to me, Jordin."

"Landon loves you. I know you two can get through this."

"I hope you're right." Jadin wiped away a lone tear. "I really hope you're right."

Landon took an empty seat at the bar, although he did not drink. He was going a bit stir-crazy in his suite, so he figured he would come down to the lobby. He originally thought about going off-site to eat, but he really wasn't hungry.

He ordered a club soda. Landon had not felt this heartsick since the day Jadin walked out of his life. It had taken a lot of effort to pull himself together, but he did it.

He would do it again.

"I'll have a white wine, please."

Landon looked up from his club soda. "Janice, what are you doing here?"

"I overheard you tell someone on the phone that you were staying here. I figured things must not be going so well in your marriage. I thought you could use a friend."

Landon shook his head. "I won't be good company."

"You're a really nice person. You don't deserve whatever this is." Janice sat down beside him at the bar. The clingy dress she wore left nothing to the imagination.

Landon knew exactly what was on her mind, but he was going to have to disappoint her. He had no interest in Janice. His heart yearned for Jadin.

The bartender handed her a glass of wine. As she reached for it, her arm brushed against Landon's hand. Their gazes collided.

Landon shifted in his seat, keeping his distance. "Janice, you really shouldn't have come here."

"Why not? I thought we were becoming friends."

"Let's not play games, Janice. You didn't come here to be my friend—not dressed like that. You came here with an agenda, but it's not going to work. I'm a married man."

*"Living in a hotel?* It doesn't sound like you're going to married much longer. Landon, I haven't known you long, but I know you well enough to know that if you're here, your marriage is over."

She moved closer to him. Lowering her voice to a whisper, she said, "I'm not going to play games with you. I've wanted you from the moment I laid eyes on you, Landon. We would be so good together."

"Janice, this is inappropriate."

She giggled. "I won't tell anybody. It'll be our little secret."

"Janice, I need you to understand something. I don't get involved with people I work with, and despite my staying here temporarily, I am still a married man."

She smoothed a dark tendril of hair behind her ear. "So, you're not attracted to me? Not even a tiny bit?"

"You are a beautiful woman, but my heart belongs to one woman."

Janice's impeccably groomed eyebrows shot up beneath her perfectly trimmed and blow-dried fringe. "If that's true…why are you here and not with her? Trying to work things out."

"It's complicated," Landon responded.

"Well, if I were you and I loved someone as much as you love Jadin, I would go home. You can't make a marriage work living apart. Do yourself a favor and fight for your marriage." Janice took a sip of her wine. "I guess you won't be my mentor after this."

"No, I won't. I was never going to do it. As I said, Trudy Mims would be a great mentor."

She stayed until she finished her wine. "Enjoy your weekend, Deputy Prosecutor. I'll see you on Monday."

He smiled. "See you then."

Landon left the bar and went up to his suite. He lay across the bed, a whirlwind of emotions washing over him. He loved Jadin and he was heartsick without her.

She had accused him of wanting the divorce because of Janice.

He sat up. Jadin was upset because she'd seen him having dinner with her. She thought *he* was leaving her for someone else.

Landon drew up the petition because he thought Jadin wanted to be with Michael. If that were true, then why would she have gotten so upset?

He muttered a curse. What if he'd been wrong about everything?

# Chapter 19

Landon left his suite and took the elevator down to the lobby. He had a breakfast meeting with the staff and wanted to get to the office early. He made a quick stop at a café inside the Alexander-DePaul Hotel. Trudy raved about the gourmet bagels and cream cheese there, so he thought he would pick up some for their meeting.

"Landon Trent," Michael greeted. "I need to know. What's wrong with you, man?"

Turning around to face his nemesis, he responded, "Excuse me?"

"I don't understand you," Michael said. "You come all the way to Charleston and make this grand display of wanting your wife back. Now that you have her, you're ready to discard your family like yesterday's trash."

Landon's mood quickly veered to anger. "The last thing I'm going to do is discuss my marriage with you."

Michael shrugged in nonchalance. "Okay, fine. If you don't want Jadin…even though she loves you, then—"

Landon cut him off by asking, "What are you talking about?"

"I came back here to get my girl, but Jadin made it very clear that she's in love with *you*. She wants to be with you, Landon, even though I tried to convince her it was a bad idea."

"Oh, is that what you were doing at Battery Park?" Landon asked. "Trying to convince my wife to leave me?"

"Hey, it worked for you, didn't it? You just waltzed into town and she went running straight into your arms. I figured I'd just do to you what you did to me."

"Did you think kissing her was the way to go?"

Michael looked at him. "Oh, she told you about that?"

"She didn't have to tell me," Landon responded. "I saw you two at the park. I was there."

"Is that what *this* is all about?" He shook his head. "Man… I kissed her, and Jadin set me straight about it. Landon, you have nothing to worry about from me."

"Then why were you at the house yesterday?"

He gave a short laugh. "What are you doing? Stalking her now?"

"No, I went there to talk to Jadin, but when I saw you, I decided to leave."

"Without talking to her?" He shook his head. "I thought you were smart. Look, like I told you, I was trying to convince her that she'd made the wrong choice, but she told me off good, so I left." Michael stole a glance at his watch. "I need to catch a flight, but I'ma say this to you. Landon, she doesn't need all this unnecessary stress with her pregnancy."

"Her what?"

"She's pregnant." Michael looked surprised. "Didn't she tell you?"

"I didn't give her much of a chance," Landon said, putting a hand to his mouth.

"If I were you...I'd go straighten things out with Jadin before I lost her for good."

"Michael, just so that we're on the same page, from this moment forward, I want you to keep your hands and your lips off my wife."

"You have my word. You know, I never really believed in soul mates, but I believe that Jadin is yours."

"I know she is," Landon said. "From the moment I first saw her, I knew she was the woman God created just for me."

"Then you need to act like it. Go get your wife."

Landon shook Michael's hand. "Thank you."

Remorse tasted sour in his mouth. Landon had been so brutal to Jadin. Guilt also danced across his heart over the fact that he had no idea that his own wife was pregnant. The nausea, dizziness and passing out—it had never occurred to him that Jadin might be carrying a child—his child.

He went by the house, but it was empty, so he drove to Austin's house. He had gotten the text about Bree having the baby. He stopped to grab a card and some flowers.

Austin greeted him at the door. "Hey, Landon. I'm glad you're here. I've been wanting to talk to you."

"Can we table our conversation until later?" he responded. "I really need to see Jadin. She wasn't home, so I thought maybe she'd be over here with Bree and the baby. I need to talk to my wife."

"Your soon-to-be ex-wife, you mean."

"Austin, I'm going to be honest with you. I messed up and I need to fix it. I saw Jadin with Michael at Battery Park. It looked like...he kissed her, and I thought..."

"You assumed she wanted to be with Michael and not you," Austin finished for him. "The same way she thinks you're interested in another woman."

"She saw me having dinner with our new prosecutor, but it was not the way it might have looked..." his voice died. "I never should have based my decision on assumptions. I should've talked to her about what I saw."

"I agree."

"I overreacted and now I might lose her and my child because of it. If you know where she is, please tell me."

"You know she's pregnant?"

"Michael told me. I ran into him earlier."

"Right now, I'm not so sure you deserve my sister," Austin said. "Running away is not the way to handle problems."

"I know that," Landon said. "My heart felt ripped in two at the idea that she wanted to be with Michael. But I love Jadin enough to let her go, Austin. I wanted her to be happy, even if it wasn't with me. I wasn't able to do that before. I told myself it was selfish to force her to stay in a marriage she didn't want to be in." His eyes grew wet with tears. "I love her so much. If I'd known the real story behind what I witnessed...I never would have had those papers drawn up."

"Are you sure you want to be with my sister? I need you to think hard about this, Landon. See, Jadin doesn't need you—she's got me, her sister…the whole DuGrandpre family."

"I know that, Austin. She's the only woman I've ever wanted, and that hasn't changed. I know I messed up, but it came from a pure place. I wanted her to be happy even if it wasn't with me."

After a moment, Austin said, "She's staying at the Jekyll Island Club Resort. If I were you, I'd leave now. Just show up. I'll get her room number and text it to you."

"Thank you, Austin." He handed him the card and flowers. "Congratulations on the birth of your daughter." Landon broke into a grin. "I'm going to be a father, too, and I can't wait."

He went to his car and got inside.

Landon whispered a quick prayer before heading for the highway. He was going to get his wife back. This time he vowed to never let her go.

Jadin heard a knock on the door and glanced at the clock on the nightstand. That was quick, she thought. She had ordered room service not even a good ten minutes ago.

She opened the door and gasped. "Landon…"

"Can I come in, please?"

Blocking his entrance, she stood there, arms folded across her chest. "We don't have anything to talk about. You said everything when you served me with divorce papers."

"We need to talk about that."

Jadin shook her head. "No, we don't. I came down

here to forget about everything going on in my life just for a few days. Landon, your being here would add more stress, so I need you to leave. I need this time to myself."

"I don't want a divorce."

"It's too late now," she responded.

"You've already filed them."

Instead of answering his question, Jadin said, "Goodbye, Landon."

"What about the baby?"

There was a brief silence.

"Is that why you have this sudden change of heart?" Jadin asked. She had hoped to keep her pregnancy from him just a bit longer. "Landon, I won't keep you from your child, if that's what you're worried about, but I'm not going to stay in a loveless marriage."

"Can I please come inside? I don't really want to discuss our relationship from the hallway."

"That's more than you gave me."

"I guess I deserve that."

"That and more," Jadin uttered, but against her better judgment, she stepped aside to allow him to enter the room.

Once they were seated, Landon said, "I never wanted a divorce, Jadin. I thought you wanted out of the marriage."

Stunned, she asked, "What gave you that idea?"

"I saw you with Michael at Battery Park. When I saw him kiss you, I misread the situation and that's why I drew up the petition. In my mind, I was giving you what you wanted—freedom to be with the man you loved."

"Why didn't you say something?"

"I was jealous, hurt, angry..."

"I don't want to be with Michael," Jadin said. "I told him that same day."

"I know," Landon responded. "I ran into Michael this morning and he cleared up everything for me. I feel really bad over the way I treated you—that's why I came down here."

"He's the one who told you about the baby?"

"Yes, but only because he thought I already knew."

Jadin settled back on the sofa, clutching a pillow to her. "I was going to tell you about the baby the night you served me with the petition for divorce."

"I did go by the house to see you, but when I saw Michael was there, I changed my mind. I really thought you wanted him. I'm so sorry, Jadin."

A loud knock cut off further conversation.

"I ordered some dinner," she said as she got up and navigated toward the door.

When the server left, they continued their conversation.

Jadin sliced into her hamburger. "Are you hungry? We can split this."

"I'm fine."

"When I brought up the woman I saw you with, you allowed me to believe the worst."

"Her name is Janice and she's a new prosecutor. She'd been assigned to shadow me that week. All those nights I told you I was working, Jadin, I was, and I was alone. She bought me dinner that night to show her gratitude. She asked me to be her mentor, but I turned her down."

"From where I stood, she was acting more like your

date and not a coworker," Jadin said. "She had other interests in mind."

"I know," Landon said. "Janice came to the hotel last night. I was in the bar—"

"You don't drink."

"I had club soda."

Jadin wiped her mouth with her napkin. "So, what happened?"

"She came on to me," Landon said. "I turned her down. Made it clear that I was still a married man. Jadin, I'm so sorry."

She looked at him. "Landon, I love you. I realized months ago that marrying Michael would've been a huge mistake. If I still had any kind of feelings for him, I never would've given myself to you. I wouldn't be pregnant right now." She paused for a moment, then said, "I thought we could talk about anything…good or bad. Now I have to wonder."

"I was so hurt, Jadin, seeing the two of you together. I didn't want to force you to stay with me if your heart belonged to someone else. I thought I was being gallant, if you want to know the truth." He pressed a hand to his chest. "But inside here, I felt like I was dying."

"Landon, love is not enough. There has to be trust between us, and from what happened… You didn't trust me."

"Sweetheart, I do trust you. That's why it hurt so much. I promise you that I won't ever make this mistake again."

"You say you trust me, but you gave up on us without checking to see if what you thought was the truth. I must be honest. It makes me wonder if you're really in for the whole till-death-do-us-part."

"Can I ask one thing of you?"

She boldly met his gaze. "What is that?"

"Spend this weekend with me," Landon said. "Let me prove to you that we belong together."

After a long silence, she said, "Do you actually think we can work this out in a couple of days?"

"No, but it's a good start."

Jadin broke into a smile. "You sure you don't want this other half?"

"You eat, sweetheart."

She bit into the burger.

"How have you been feeling?" Landon inquired. "Have you had any morning sickness?"

She chewed and swallowed. "Not really. I feel nauseous every now and then, but that's about it… Thank goodness. Jordin was really sick when she was pregnant."

"When is the baby due?"

"In seven months."

He smiled. "I'm going to be a father. I want you to know that I feel awful. I should've known that you were pregnant."

"How could you know?" Jadin asked. "I didn't even know. I was on the Pill. I had to get them switched. Apparently, it takes time for my body to adjust." She broke into a smile. "I know this pregnancy wasn't planned, but are you sure you're ready for daddy duty?"

"Yeah, I am," Landon said. "My dad and I had a great relationship until he passed away. His brother stepped up to make sure I didn't miss out on things like sports. It was hard for my uncle to be at every one of my games because of his job, but when he could, he was there."

She reached out and took his hand. "I have no doubts that you'll be a great father."

"You're just not sure I'll be a good husband."

Jadin touched his cheek. "I know you're a good husband, silly. What I have doubts about is how we are going to handle the hard stuff that comes along? I got scared and I ran. You did the same thing. What does this say about us?"

"That we're experiencing what most people go through early in their marriages. This is the first time that we've lived as husband and wife. I guess it's normal." Landon looked at her. "Please tell me that you didn't file the divorce petition."

"I was going to, but my mom told me to wait. She told me not to do it until I had a clear head." Jadin pointed to his finger. "You're still wearing your ring."

"I couldn't bring myself to take it off." Landon picked up her left hand. "You still have yours on, too."

"Same reason," Jadin murmured.

"I need to know what you saw in Michael. You accepted his proposal of marriage. Why?"

"I bought into the whole we-are-so-right-for-each-other speech he gave me. When I left you, I knew that I would never love anybody the way I loved you, Landon. So I wasn't looking for a deep, intense love like we shared. I was just looking for someone who would care for me, respect me and be good to me. Michael and I weren't a perfect fit, but it worked and so I settled. But then you came back into my life." Jadin smiled. "You rescued me. You showed me that what I have with you is perfect."

"What we share is real, Jadin. I promise that I am committed to our marriage for all of eternity."

"That's a long time," she responded. "You're sure about this?"

"I was sure that day in Vegas, when you became my wife."

# Chapter 20

Saturday morning, Jadin woke up to find Landon had already ordered breakfast for them.

"What would you like to do today?" he asked her.

"We can go the beach, or we can go horseback riding. I know how much you love history, so we can spend some time touring the Jekyll Island Club, which was the playground for J. P. Morgan, Marshall Field, Joseph Pulitzer and William Vanderbilt."

"Really?"

Jadin nodded. "This island used to be their winter retreat."

"Well, it's beautiful here," Landon said. "I didn't get to see a whole lot yesterday. I was more focused on getting to you."

"My parents call this one of Georgia's best-kept secrets. My mother was born in Brunswick. Her parents moved to Charleston when she was ten, but she spent a lot of summers in this area with her grandparents."

"I'd like to go to St. Simons Island while I'm here," Landon said.

"Okay." A smile tugging at her lips. Jadin then inquired, "How did you sleep?"

"The sofa was comfortable enough."

"Did you really expect me to welcome you back in my bed with open arms?"

"I was hoping so," Landon confessed. "But I know you better than that, so I knew you wouldn't."

"Then why didn't you know that I'd never go back to Michael after giving myself to you? I'm not the kind of girl who jumps from man to man like that."

"Jadin, I reacted over a broken heart. I was blinded by jealousy and I'm sorry. Please tell me that we can get past this."

"I guess we'll find out this weekend."

She took him via horseback to her favorites spots on the island.

"I haven't been on a horse since Uncle Tim and I went to Montana. We spent a week at this ranch. It was pretty cool."

After spending the day touring the island, they drove to Brunswick to dine at Zachary's Seafood and Steak. Both she and Landon chose the crab cake sandwich with rémoulade sauce.

Later, Jadin and Landon drove across the bridge to St. Simons Island, where they walked off their lunch.

"There's so much history on this island…in this area," Landon said. "I've always wanted to come to see where the Battle of the Bloody Marsh took place and Fort Frederica."

"You have a real interest in war history," Jadin responded.

"I do. I guess I'm always trying to really understand why they happened."

She took a picture of Christ Church with the camera on her iPhone. The small church was surrounded by mossy grass and sat under towering oak trees. "This is one of the oldest churches in Georgia."

"The fifty-fourth Massachusetts infantry actually spent some time on this island. I read some of the letters from Colonel Robert Shaw about his time here."

"*Glory* is one of my favorite movies," Jadin said. "I've always wanted to go to a Civil War reenactment."

"We can do that," Landon responded. "I've gone to a couple with my uncle. We had a wonderful time. When all the kids are a bit older, I'd like to take them to one. It's a great way to learn history."

Later, back in their suite, Landon wrapped his arms around her.

He kept Jadin there in front of him, his mouth blazing a hot trail against the sensitive skin of her neck. "Do you have any idea of how much I've missed you? How bad I wanted you?" He unzipped her dress, which she let fall to the floor in a puddle.

The feel of Landon's hands touching her so intimately made Jadin shudder with pleasure and made her toes curl into the soft carpet. Jadin turned to face him as his hands explored the curve of her back. Her skin tingled wherever he touched her.

Landon looked at her with hungry eyes, feasting on her, taking in her nearly naked body. She had never felt more desirable. More beautiful.

"You're so gorgeous."

Jadin attempted to unbutton his shirt, but her fingers were useless. In the end, Landon whipped it off over his head and tossed it onto a nearby chair. She undid his belt and trousers. He stepped out of them.

He crushed her mouth to his as his hands went back to her hips, holding her against him.

"Sweetheart, are you sure about this?"

"I want you to make love to me all night long."

Landon's lips parted and claimed her tongue. Hungrily, they devoured each other's lips, and Jadin melted into his passionate embrace. Her entire body pulsated in anticipation.

He kissed her gently on the throat as he traced his fingertips across her lips. The gentle massage sent currents of desire through her.

Their chemistry had always been electrifying.

Jadin's last thought before they made love was just how perfect she and Landon were together.

"I love you."

Jadin stroked his jaw as she gazed into his eyes. "I love you, too," she whispered.


"Ready to go home?" Landon asked.

"We drove in separate cars."

"I rented mine. I came down with the expectation that we'd be traveling home together."

"Really?"

"I was praying," he said with a chuckle. "I don't think I've ever prayed so hard."

When they made it to Savannah, Landon said, "I'd like to make a little detour. I don't know about you but I'm not ready to go back home."

"So you want to spend a few days here in Savannah?"

"No," he responded. "We're going to the airport. From there, we're going to fly to Jamaica."

"You're kidding."

Landon gave her a sidelong glance. "I'm serious. We need some time together, away from everybody."

"But I'm supposed to go back to work on Monday."

"I spoke with your father. You have the week off. Oh, I have your passport, too. It was in the safe with mine. When I left the house, I took it with me."

Jadin nodded in understanding. "When did you plan this little side trip?"

"Before I left Charleston," Landon confessed. "I just wasn't sure it would actually happen, but it was a risk I was willing to take."


"Jamaica, Jamaica. Here we are," Jadin said with an appreciative grin as she entered their suite. She could not believe she was actually here with Landon, after everything that had happened.

Landon placed their bags near the closet.

"It's a good thing I always overpack," Jadin said. "Or I'd have to do a lot of shopping."

"I'm sure you're going to pick up a couple of things while we're here anyway."

She laughed. "Probably."

Her eyes scanned their suite. "This is beautiful. I love the view of the ocean from the bedroom."

Jadin made herself comfortable on the plush sofa in the room. "When I left Charleston, I was looking for a quiet weekend to think and sit on the balcony alone, watching the waves and reading on my Kindle. Now

I'm here in Jamaica with you on a romantic vacation. If I was a swooning type of woman…"

Landon chuckled. "Every now and then, we need to do something impulsive—it doesn't always have to be preplanned."

"The last impulsive thing I did was marry you," Jadin said.

He sat down beside her. "It wasn't a mistake. It *isn't* a mistake." He pressed his hand to her stomach. "This baby is proof of that."

"That's one of the reasons I love you so much—you always know the right things to say."

Jadin pointed to the brochure on the coffee table. "They have a really nice buffet at the restaurant downstairs. From the pictures, it's a gorgeous view. The least we could do is enjoy it and listen to the sea waves."

"Is that your way of saying you're hungry?"

She smiled. "In the nicest way possible."

Landon was more than thrilled that Jadin had agreed to come to Jamaica with him. His uncle's recommendation had not disappointed. The hotel had four freshwater pools, as well as a sunbed, shower and towel service. The main pool had two built-in Jacuzzis and a swim-up bar. There was also an adults-only pool, which he and Jadin both enjoyed.

He thought that every time he saw her sexy body in a swimsuit, he would go crazy. Every inch of his body reacted to her presence. Even though she was carrying his child, she was still fabulous in every way.

They both found the ocean waves calming. Sometimes they would listen in silence, other times they shared what was on their minds.

"Thank you," she told him when she swam over. "I'm glad we came here. Spending time with you like this has been perfect. I agree that we really needed some time away from work and everybody."

Landon leaned in closer to her. He could feel her breath quickening. His lips brushed hers and they locked in a passionate kiss.

They returned to the hotel after spending most of the day at the beach.

Landon came out of the shower as Jadin finished blow-drying her hair. The water pressure was amazing in the hotel. She'd had her shower first.

"You look beautiful," he said, his eyes penetrating her as he grinned.

Jadin smiled. "I'm wearing a towel."

"So am I," he responded in a husky tone.

They gazed hungrily into each other's eyes.

Slowly and seductively, her towel slid downward. "Oops…"

Grinning, Landon followed suit.

When they returned home from Jamaica, Landon moved back into the house with Jadin.

He pretended to be engrossed in the legal brief he had prepared on his laptop when Jadin walked out of the bathroom, dressed for their date night. She was wearing a sexy black dress with a scooped neckline that showed off her body spectacularly. Jadin had on high heels and her hair was pulled up and artfully arranged in a mass of curls, a style that managed to look both casual and elegant at the same time.

Her eye makeup highlighted the depth and shape of her brown eyes, and the mascara she was wearing made her eyelashes look like miniature black fans. Her lips were full and glossy from a shimmering lipstick.

"You look stunning," he said.

Jadin smiled. "Thank you."

She grabbed her purse. "I'm ready. We need to leave now to make our dinner reservations."

"Yes, ma'am." Landon closed his laptop and swung his legs off the bed.

Jadin and Landon dined at High Cotton on East Bay Street forty-five minutes later.

"I'm going to have to add this place to my list of favorite restaurants," Landon told her. "When you suggested the jalapeño rémoulade with the crab cakes, I wasn't sure if I'd like it, but it was delicious. It had just enough kick without being too spicy." Landon's eyes traveled the room, taking in the rich jewel tones. "This is a very nice place."

"I'm glad you liked it," she responded. "I would have ordered the same thing, but I've decided to stay away from really spicy food during this pregnancy."

"I turned in my resignation today," Landon announced.

Jadin laid down her fork. "Are you going back to the Secret Service?"

"How would you feel about it?"

"I'd be okay with your decision," she responded. "When you first joined, all I knew about them was that they guarded the president and other diplomats. I didn't realize that they were involved with investigating bank fraud, computer fraud and crimes dealing with intellectual property. I'd be more comfortable if you stayed off protective detail, though."

"One thing I've learned through this is that my work

isn't the most important thing in my life. The most important thing in my life is you, Jadin. I'm not going back to the Secret Service. Like I told you before, the long hours of unpaid overtime—that's not a benefit to me. I would rather spend that time with you and our child. I don't want to miss ball games, ballet recitals… all the special moments that we can't ever get back." Landon lifted his head, looked into her eyes and whispered, "You're everything to me, Jadin."

"I believe you," she said, her eyes bright with tears. "I don't want to miss another minute of life with you."

Jadin took a sip of her iced tea. "It never ceases to amaze me how in tune we are with one another. I've actually been thinking about my priorities, as well," Jadin said. "Now that we're starting a family, I'm going to talk to my dad about switching to family law. I don't want the demands that come with being a criminal lawyer. Austin's very good at balancing the job and family. I know I can probably do it, too, but I want to spend as much time with my children as possible."

Landon smiled. "What do you think about my coming on board?"

Her eyes widened in surprise. "You mean coming to work at the law firm?"

"Yes."

"Landon, I'd love it." Jadin was beyond happy.

"How do you think your father will feel about it?"

"He's spending the day with Mom tomorrow, so we can drive out there and talk to him. I'm sure he'll be thrilled." Jadin wiped her mouth with her napkin. "I need to talk to my mom anyway. I want to tell her that we've decided to have a real wedding."

"I think it's important for us to renew our vows. I

know we meant them back then, but I believe that we have grown a lot. This time we'll have a much better understanding when we say them."

"I agree," Jadin said.

She could not recall later how they got to the bedroom. It seemed one minute they were kissing in the middle of the living room, and the next they were in the bed. All she could remember was the thrill of Landon's mouth fused to hers. His desire for her was unending.

She could feel the hardened heat of him as Landon crushed her mouth beneath his.

"I want you naked," he whispered against her mouth, his hand warm and firm on her hips.

Jadin broke away long enough to say, "I'm going to need some help with this zipper."

## Chapter 21

"Well, this is a wonderful surprise," Eleanor said when Jadin and Landon walked into the dining room, where her parents were having lunch. "Are you two hungry?"

"We grabbed something to eat before we came here," Jadin responded.

Etienne wiped his mouth, then looked at Landon over the rims of his glasses. "I hope this means that you've come to your senses."

"Yes, sir, I have."

"That's one of the reasons we came by," Jadin said. "Landon and I want to renew our vows. We want to have a wedding, reception…the works."

Eleanor beamed. "That makes me so happy."

Jadin took Landon's hand. "We need to do it in the next month or so."

"Hon, we can't plan a proper wedding so quickly."

"Mom, I don't want or need anything extravagant."

Landon looked at Etienne. "I want you to know that Jadin makes me very happy and I never want to risk losing her again. And I'm making a career change and will be resigning from my position at the prosecutor's office."

"So, what are you planning to do for a job, son?"

"I'm hoping there's a place for me with your firm."

"Crossing over to the dark side, I see. You think you're ready for that?"

"Dad...stop teasing," Jadin said.

"I want Landon to really think about his decision. He has worked in law enforcement and as a prosecutor. We work to defend our clients, guilty or innocent. Not everyone can be a criminal attorney."

"You're right," Landon responded. "I've given it a lot of thought and I'd prefer to specialize in family law."

"So would I," Jadin interjected. "I know I asked to take on criminal cases, but now that we're having this baby, neither one of us wants to spend long hours at the office, preparing for trials. We want as much time with our child and each other as possible."

"I'm assuming you're no longer going to take litigation cases, either."

Jadin shook her head. "I'd rather not."

"That's fine," Etienne said. "We just hired a new attorney who wants to specialize in litigation. Carl, Daniel and Austin can handle the criminal cases for now."

"Thank you, Daddy."

Jadin exchanged a smile with her mother. She was excited about taking this leap of faith with Landon. She knew that being with him would make her life happier than she'd ever dreamed possible.

* * *

Kai, Amya and Emery spent the weekend with them. Jadin was not sure who was more excited—the kids or Landon. He had a full itinerary planned.

After breakfast, they spent the morning hours at Battery Park. He had even bought bicycles for them.

"Now we have two bikes," Kai said.

"I wanted you to have one whenever you spend the weekend with us," Landon explained.

"Cool..." she murmured. "We should have two of all of our toys. One for home and one for your house."

Jadin laughed. "Nice try, Kai."

Amya took her by the hand. "I like Landon. He's really nice."

"I'm glad to hear you say that." She smiled at her young cousin. "I like him, too."

"That's 'cause he's your *boo*."

"Where are you getting this stuff from?"

"Mama calls Daddy her *boo* sometimes. It's because she loves him."

Jadin awarded her a smile. "That's actually a good point of reference. Yes, Landon is my *boo*."

After lunch, they took the kids to a petting zoo, where they fed, held and cared for pets as if they were their own. She was amazed over the way the children were so gentle with the animals.

"They're doing an excellent job with these animals," Landon whispered.

Jadin nodded in agreement. "I know Emery has been asking for a puppy. He loves dogs."

"I've never been much of an animal person," he confessed. "What about you?"

"I don't want any. I can't even take care of a plant."

She gave him a sidelong glance. "I'm good with babies, so you don't have to worry about our little one."

Landon kissed her. "I know that, sweetheart. You're going to be a wonderful mother."

"Yessss... Kiss her again," Amya said. "Kiss her again."

He did as he was instructed, then said, "I think we have a budding romantic in her."

Jadin smiled. "I don't think there's anything wrong with that at all." She thought briefly of how Michael used to ridicule her romantic ideas. She intended to make sure that never happened to Amya.

"Okay, I just cut my lunch short with my mom, so this better be good," Jadin said when she got into Landon's SUV. "Where are we going?"

"You'll see," he said cryptically. "It's a surprise."

"You know our wedding is in three weeks. There's so much that has to be done. Mom wants us to meet her at Kincaid Bakery for a cake tasting this evening."

"We'll be there," Landon interjected. "Sweetheart, relax..."

"At least I can check the invitations off the list. We had to pay a lot to get them rushed. They'll be ready tomorrow." While she talked, Jadin made notes on her iPhone.

He turned on Boom Vang Lane and parked in front of a house.

Jadin looked at him. "What are we doing here?"

"You said we needed to find a bigger house. C'mon... Let's go inside."

She smiled at the Realtor standing on the porch.

Walking into the home, they were greeted by gorgeous hardwood floors and smooth ceilings that flowed into the open living area.

"It's beautiful," Jadin murmured. "I love that it is so open. This house is perfect for family dinners." The eat-in kitchen offered granite countertops and a butler's pantry.

She fell in love with the master bedroom, which had a sitting room, bright windows, a bathroom en suite and a private porch. "Landon, I love this."

"Did you notice the tub is big enough for two people?" Landon whispered in her ear.

She laughed. "I saw that."

There were three more bedrooms. The selling point for Jadin was that the home also offered a bonus room. "We can each have an office."

"This house was meant for a family." Landon's arms tightened around her. "This is where I want to raise our kids. I want to grow old with you here."

Jadin leaned up and touched her lips to his. "I think we just bought a house."

# Chapter 22

Jadin's mother and Aunt Rochelle had everything in place for their late-September wedding. The weather was still warm enough for them to have their ceremony on the beach behind the DuGrandpre estate.

The gazebo overlooking the beautiful ocean was simply breathtaking.

*Picture perfect.*

The seats had white chair covers, and flowers adorned the entire setting. Family and friends dressed in tuxedos and bright jewel-toned dresses roamed across the manicured lawn while waiting for the ceremony to start. Classical music played undercurrent to the rush of conversation that rose and fell like waves crashing against the shore.

Inside the house, Jadin stared out the window. "Mom, everything is so beautiful. You and Aunt Rochelle did an outstanding job pulling this together in such a short time."

"I'm so glad you're happy, hon. I want this day to be as perfect as you are," Eleanor responded.

"Auntie Jay," Emery said. "I thought you was already married."

She glanced at her mother in amusement. "I am. Your uncle and I are renewing our vows. When we said them the first time, no one was there but Auntie Jo. We want to do it again with all of you here with us."

Eleanor handed Emery a satin pillow. "You are the ring bearer."

The little boy looked at it and said, "Where are the rings?"

Jadin burst into laughter.

"Oh, dear…" Eleanor murmured. "I think Rochelle has the ones that go on this pillow. Emery, you hold tight. Go sit over there."

"Yes, ma'am," he said.

Kai burst into the room. "Jadin, I just saw Landon. He looks like a prince."

"Does he now?"

She nodded. "You look like a princess." Kai twirled around in the lacy dress she was wearing. "How do I look?"

"Just gorgeous," Jadin responded. "You and Amya are going to be the cutest flower girls in Charleston."

Jadin looked at the clock. It was time for the ceremony to begin.

She could not resist a peek at her husband.

"What are you doing?" Jordin asked.

"I've been married to that man for five years. We're

renewing our vows, not getting married for the first time."

Landon stood near the pastor, looking tall, dark and gorgeous, his physique the epitome of good health. Beside him was his uncle. Jadin was thrilled that Tim and his wife had traveled here to the wedding. Everything was as it should be, she thought.

The most unforgettable romantic tune of all time, "At Last" by Etta James, played as Jadin walked down the aisle toward her future.

"I stand today in front of our family, our friends and you, my husband, to reaffirm my marriage vows. Five years ago, we stood at a tiny chapel and said vows that were written for us. Today, I am not simply taking a vow—I am giving you a promise in words that are my own.

"Landon, I love you more than I could ever have imagined, and that love is enough to overcome anything that comes our way. I love you more today because of all that we have been through and because of your willingness to move forward with renewed commitment. I promise from this day forward to love and trust you even more as time passes. I promise to be there for you when you are sick, hurt, in need of comfort or when you just want to share your day. I promise to make you feel needed and appreciated for all that you bring into my life for as long as we both live."

Landon's eyes grew wet, matching her own tear-filled gaze.

He cleared his throat, then began speaking. "On our wedding day five years ago, I made a choice. It was the most important and significant choice of my life and I made it after a great deal of consideration. On that day, I chose you to be my wife. I knew that decision was final and irrevocable. As our lives have been affected by the ebb and flow of other lives and events, there were times we chose to go in different directions. I choose to stay married not because I feel obligated, but because of my love for you. This is not because a legal document says that I am your husband, but because I still want to be by your side more than I want to be anywhere else."

He took Jadin by the hand and they turned to face their guests.

"We are here for a celebration," Jadin said.

"We rejoice that five years ago, we had the good sense to marry one other," Landon added with a grin.

Jadin glanced over at her mother and said, "Most of all, we celebrate that we are able to share this special once-in-a-lifetime occasion with the people we love most in this world."

"Like my wife said, we celebrate a dream come true, and what makes it really special is that we are able to celebrate together with you—our family and friends."

Jadin turned to face her husband once more.

"You may kiss your bride," the pastor said.

"Gladly," Landon responded with a grin. "C'mere, Mrs. Trent."

## Chapter 23

After the wedding, Landon and Jadin spent a week at the Double D Ranch in Roger's Pass, Montana, which boasted thirty-three cabins.

Jadin leaned her shoulder against a column built from a tree that had been harvested in the nearby woods, while Landon secured their horses. She never tired of the majestic pines towering toward wispy clouds floating in a clear blue sky. Behind the trees, the mountains rose, their stair-step peaks cloaked in the first snow of the season. A few yards away from them, a clear creek crowded with trout was a favorite fishing location with many of the guests.

They found a spot to spread a blanket. Clara, the manager of the ranch, had prepared a picnic basket for them.

"So, what do you think of the Double D?" Landon asked.

"I actually love it here," Jadin responded. "I'm glad

we came here instead of going to some exotic island. I enjoy trying new experiences." She took a bite of a fried drumstick.

"I love seafood, but I'm definitely not into fishing."

Jadin agreed, "Yeah, I'm not interested in catching my own food."

They finished their lunch, then rode the horses back to the ranch.

In the evenings, meals were served family-style. Everyone dined at long tables that held twelve to fourteen people, and they enjoyed simple country fare.

Landon sat across from her. He flashed her a smile.

"You two are just the cutest couple," the woman seated beside her said. "Are you two on your honeymoon?"

"We've actually been married for five and a half years," Jadin responded.

"Well, you two are a beautiful couple. My husband and I have been married forty years. You and your husband remind me of me and Dan."

"Mrs. Darling, how long have you two owned this ranch?"

"It's been in Dan's family for three generations. When his daddy passed on, we decided to do some renovations and turn it into a resort. My Dan was never a fan of growing things out of the ground, but he loved the animals."

After dinner, Landon and Jadin sat on the porch of their cabin, soaking in the moonlight.

"I can't remember the last time I ate so much," he said, rubbing his belly.

"Everything was delicious." Jadin stopped rocking. "Are you really gonna enter the chili cook-off?"

Landon nodded. "I think I can win."

She smiled. "Really? Why are you so confident? You're a good cook and all…"

"You sound like you don't have faith in me, sweetheart."

"I have faith in you—I just want to know why you're feeling so confident about this chili cook-off."

"Because we're going to call around and collect chili recipes. Then we're going to pick the one we think will beat out everybody else."

Jadin agreed. "I'll call my mom and Aubrie. You know my cousin probably has, like, ten different ways to make chili."

"I'll call Uncle Tim. His chili is pretty good."

Jadin reached over and took Landon's hand. "Teamwork."

At the foot of the stone walkway, Jadin veered left to the area designated for the chili cook-off. It looked like hundreds of people were on the grounds for the annual contest hosted by the Double D Ranch. She had no doubt that hundreds more would venture in and out throughout the afternoon.

Folding tables had been set up for the cook-off contestants, with two entries per table. The ranch provided single-burner butane cookstoves. Everything else, from kettles to ingredients, was up to the contestants.

Jadin and Landon decided to enter just for the fun of it, although he really believed he had a chance at winning. He had gone to town to buy the supplies and ingredients needed for their recipe.

She was surprised when she saw the guest named Matt, who was staying in the cottage next to theirs, stirring a huge pot and chatting with his tablemate. *He must be a regular*, she decided. He had to have brought everything he needed to make his chili with him.

"Hey, sweetheart," Landon said. "I think I have everything."

"Okay, so we have four recipes. I know which one I think we should go with, but I want to see which one you're going to choose."

"I think we should use my mother's recipe," Landon said. "She's from Texas and, man...that woman could cook some chili."

Jadin laughed. "That's my pick, as well."

He kissed her. "Let's do this."

By the time the judges came around, they were ready.

"So, tell me about this recipe," one of the judges said.

"This is my mother's recipe," Landon said. "She was born and raised in Texas. This chili is what Texans call a 'Bowl o' Red.' You don't put beans or tomatoes in it— just beef, homemade chili paste and a few flavorings. The key is letting the chili simmer to avoid evaporating the sauce before the beef is tender."

Jadin ladled portions into plastic bowls and gave one to each judge. She studied their faces as they sampled the chili, but their expressions were unreadable.

The judges moved on to their tablemate.

She looked up at him. "I've really had a wonderful time here with you. I've never ever been on a ranch before, so this is an incredible experience."

"I'm glad I'm able to share this with you, sweetheart. My uncle and I love coming here, but I wanted to bring you, too. It's relaxing to me."

"I can see that."

Later that evening, they sat on the floor in front of

the fireplace, admiring Landon's trophy for winning the chili cook-off.

"Congratulations, baby."

"We're a team. We did this together."

Jadin leaned her back against him. "Everything about my life is perfect. It just doesn't get any better than what we have now."

"Oh, I don't know about that," Landon responded. "Turn around and face me."

She did as he instructed.

Unable to resist kissing her, Landon crushed his lips against hers. Grabbing her neck to pull her closer, he pushed his tongue against her lips, demanding entrance.

Jadin's breath quickened.

Liquid heat began pooling in her core as Landon deepened the kiss, pulling her so close that she could hardly tell where her body left off and his began. Her hands slipped up behind his neck.

Jadin smiled up at him, reveling in the promise of love, life and a future that looked brighter than any she could have imagined. "I thank the Lord for another chance with you," she whispered.

\* \* \* \* \*

**Soulful and sensual romance featuring
multicultural characters.**

Look for brand-new Kimani stories
in special 2-in-1 volumes starting March 2019.

Available March 5, 2019

**LOVE IN SAN FRANCISCO & UNCONDITIONALLY**
by Shirley Hailstock and Janice Sims

**A TASTE OF PASSION & AMBITIOUS SEDUCTION**
by Chloe Blake and Nana Prah

**PLEASURE AT MIDNIGHT & HIS PICK
FOR PASSION**
by Pamela Yaye and Synithia Williams

**BECAUSE YOU LOVE ME & JOURNEY TO
MY HEART**
by Monica Richardson and Terra Little

# Get 4 FREE REWARDS!

## We'll send you 2 FREE Books plus 2 FREE Mystery Gifts.

**Harlequin® Desire** books feature heroes who have it all: wealth, status, incredible good looks... everything but the right woman.

FREE Value Over **$20**

*Though heir to his family's international empire,
Leonardo Astacio chose to make his name in the legal
arena. Now he's up for a partnership and must work
with his competition—ambitious attorney
Kamilla Gordon—to win their firm a deep-pockets
client. In Aspen, the simmering attraction they've been
fighting boils over. But when they uncover corruption
that reaches to the highest levels, can passionate rivals
become lovers for life?*

*Read on for a sneak peek at
Ambitious Seduction,
the next exciting installment in
The Astacios series by Nana Prah!*

Once she'd heard the rumor about Singleton Financial
wanting to find another firm to represent their conglomeration,
she'd dived for their information. After being trusted to
work with them—although with Leonardo—within the past
year, she felt obligated to encourage them to stay. What had
happened to make them want to leave? It couldn't have been
the work she and Leonardo had done for them; they'd been
happy customers two months ago.

She wouldn't focus on what else had transpired during
that time, but her skin heated at the memory that was trying

to make its way to the forefront of her mind. Soon she'd be face-to-face with the man she'd been avoiding. They'd never been friends, so it hadn't been that hard to stay away. And yet her body still betrayed her on a daily basis and longed for the boar's touch.

Shaking off the biggest mistake of her life, she zoned in on her career. If she could maintain Singleton Financial as a client, she'd definitely be made partner. No way would she allow the muscle-bound Astacio to snatch the chance away from her.

Once again she wondered why he even worked for the firm. His family possessed more money than Oprah Winfrey and Bill Gates combined. He could've gone to work for his family, started his own law firm or even retired. Jealousy roared to life at how easy his life had been.

A buzz from her phone brought her out of her musings just in time to prepare her for the bear who banged her poor door against the wall before storming in. Their erotic encounter hadn't changed him a bit.

Canting her head, she presented a smile sweet enough for him to develop cavities. "How may I help you, Leonardo?" For a rather uptight law firm, they held an open policy about calling people by their first names, although most of the employees called him Mr. Astacio out of terror. She'd rather scrub toilets at an office building again, a job she'd had in high school.

He stopped in front of her desk and braced his hands on it. "You have something that belongs to me."

A thrill shimmied down her spine at being so close to him. Ignoring the way his baritone voice sounded even huskier than normal, she looked around her shared office, glad to find they were alone so they could fight toe-to-toe. "What's that?"

"Don't play games." He pointed to his chest, about to speak again, when an adorable sneeze slipped out. Followed by four more. So the big bad wolf had a cold. From the gossip mill, she knew he never got sick. Detested doing so.

She got to her feet and walked around her desk to the door. She used it as a fan to air the room out. "Since I can't open the windows, I'd prefer if you didn't share your nasty germs with me."

His clenched, broad jaw didn't scare her. Especially considering how his upturned nose now held a tinge of red after blowing it. The man had a monopoly on sexy with his large dark brown eyes and sharp cheekbones. His tailored suit hugged a muscular body she'd jump hurdles to get reacquainted with if he wasn't such an arrogant ass. *And my competition for financial freedom. Mustn't forget that.*

Leonardo held out his hand. "Hand over the file. It's mine."

She'd worn her favorite suit to work, so she had an extra dose of power on her side. Although her outfit wasn't tailored like his, she'd spent more money on the form-flattering dark plum skirt suit than she had on three of her others combined. Kamilla perched a hand on her hip and hitched her upper body forward in a challenge. "Who says?"

"I do."

Tapping her finger against her chin, she shrugged. "Well, that's all the verification I need. I'll give it to you." She sashayed to her desk and sat on the edge. "Right after I'm finished analyzing it."

*Don't miss* Ambitious Seduction
*by Nana Prah, available March 2019*
*wherever Harlequin® Kimani Romance™*
*books and ebooks are sold.*

Want to give in to temptation with
steamy tales of irresistible desire?

Check out **Harlequin® Presents®,
Harlequin® Desire** and
**Harlequin® Kimani™ Romance** books!

**New books available every month!**

**CONNECT WITH US AT:**

Facebook.com/groups/HarlequinConnection

 Facebook.com/HarlequinBooks

 Twitter.com/HarlequinBooks

 Instagram.com/HarlequinBooks

 Pinterest.com/HarlequinBooks

ReaderService.com

**HARLEQUIN®**

**ROMANCE WHEN
YOU NEED IT**

PGENRE2018

Need an adrenaline rush from nail-biting tales
(and irresistible males)?

Check out **Harlequin Intrigue®**
and **Harlequin® Romantic Suspense** books!

**New books available every month!**

---

**CONNECT WITH US AT:**

Facebook.com/groups/HarlequinConnection

 Facebook.com/HarlequinBooks

Twitter.com/HarlequinBooks

 Instagram.com/HarlequinBooks

 Pinterest.com/HarlequinBooks

ReaderService.com

**ROMANCE WHEN
YOU NEED IT**

SGENRE2018

# *Love Harlequin romance?*

## DISCOVER.

Be the first to find out about promotions,
news and exclusive content!

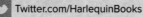

Facebook.com/HarlequinBooks

Twitter.com/HarlequinBooks

Instagram.com/HarlequinBooks

Pinterest.com/HarlequinBooks

ReaderService.com

## EXPLORE.

Sign up for the Harlequin e-newsletter and
download a free book from any series at
**TryHarlequin.com.**

## CONNECT.

Join our Harlequin community to share
your thoughts and connect with other
romance readers!
**Facebook.com/groups/HarlequinConnection**

**ROMANCE WHEN
YOU NEED IT**

HSOCIAL2018